I0747679

Mahatmas
and
Monsters

Kim Idynne

Copyright © 2022 Kim Idynne

All rights reserved.

ISBN: 978-1-7350798-4-4

for Zea & Sam

1

Even before he saw her face, Elias knew the woman by her scent. Two evenings ago, he had caught her trespassing in the parking lot of the Woodlands Business Center. He had even tried to bite her.

She carried the scent of fragrant incense and the heavy smell of oil, and her short hair was infused with the leavings of a floral shampoo. Beneath those odors Elias detected the basic musk of her body, an oil-and-woods smell of someone who spent a lot of time outdoors—and somehow, even on the first encounter, that smell was familiar to him. Her face, too, affected him with a strange sense of recognition. Her short hair had been badly cut with an unflattering fringe of bangs across the top, trimmed too high above her large brown eyes. It was the eyes that struck some remembered chord in Elias.

On that first evening, the young woman had regarded him with caution, as ladies sometimes did. Elias could usually find a way to get their guard down, but with her, he hadn't had a chance. Instead, she had surprised him by walking right up to him, looking him in the eye, and saying: "My friend is dead because of you. If you ever try to do that to anyone again, I will take back every drop of blood you've stolen; I will suck every last drop out of your body."

She turned away. After a startled moment, Elias lunged for her. Later, he supposed he had done so in a panic: she knew what he was, what he had done. She would warn people. The police, and others, would begin poking their noses into his business. But the woman surprised Elias again with an unexpected show of speed, sprinting across the lawn and into the woods beyond. Try as he might, he could not follow her scent. It dissipated as he trailed farther and farther behind her, until at last he gave up and gasped painfully for breath, assuring himself that he was not slow and out of shape; he simply wasn't a chaser. There were more than enough women who were drawn to him, who came to him without any effort on his part. This young woman might even turn out to be one of them; she might come back.

And she did.

Tonight, the woman caused a commotion by coming all the way through the front doors, which the inhabitants had unwisely left unlocked. Once inside, she found herself in the company of monsters: a vampire, a werewolf, and a succubus.

The Business Center, a long, square-shaped arrangement of hallways and old office spaces, served as their living quarters as well as their workplace. Elias had come up with the clever idea of getting the place re-zoned for business and residential use, so that he and his housemates could easily avoid one another. The long halls and many rooms made it less confining, while the empty lot and sprawling company lawn ensured they wouldn't be encroached on by neighbors.

Elias was in his office, sitting at his computer, when he heard Bruno's yelling and his huge feet pounding down the hall. Before he could stand up, the door burst open. "We have an intruder," Bruno panted. "Some lady just walked in and is wandering around the building."

Elias calmly rose from his seat. "I'll find her."

"Great." Bruno lifted a hand to his nose. "It's the new moon. My sniffer is useless."

"It usually is."

2

Elias didn't hurry. He headed for the front of the building, and as he approached the doors, the woman's scent brought him to a halt.

"It's her," he said.

Leitha, the so-called succubus who had only recently moved into the office complex, stood indecisively in the lobby. She was still dressed in her pajamas: a pair of cotton boxer shorts and an oversized T-shirt. "Who?" she asked.

Elias shook his head. "Some girl who was snooping around here yesterday. I'll take care of her."

He walked on, tracing the scent to the end of the hall. The woman had gone into the last room, an unused office space with an old vinyl couch and empty file cabinets. She was presumably still there; that corner of the building lacked windows.

Leitha spoke up behind him: "Which way?"

Elias gestured back the way they had come. "Circle back, will you?" he suggested. "She must be coming around that way."

Leitha did as Elias asked. She always did.

He sauntered around the corner and lingered there, listening. From where he stood, he heard the intruder's breath in the spare office, and the sound of Leitha's retreating steps.

When the succubus was out of sight, Elias entered the room. He closed the door behind him and let out a loud sigh, ensuring that the woman knew of his presence. The couch was situated against the far wall; he debated sitting there, but it would have given him a view of the intruder, who was hiding behind the tallest of the filing cabinets.

Instead, he sat in the middle of the floor and waited. Elias wasn't a chaser; he didn't like to attack. He much preferred it when his prey came to him.

The young woman's voice suddenly filled the room:

"Why are you so obsessed with killing me?"

The question startled Elias—perhaps not just the question, but the tone in which it was asked. The woman's words rang of genuine curiosity, of tranquility. It lacked the strain of terror that Elias expected of someone pursued by monsters.

He replied just as calmly: "You trespassed here. No one has tried to kill you. And I'm sure you're mistaken about your friend. I don't have the faintest idea who you were talking about."

"Of course you don't. You wouldn't have bothered to know her."

"I see. And you think I'm going to kill you?"

"You'll try," she replied. "I think you're sitting on the floor like that to pretend you're not interested in attacking me—but you followed me all the way to this room so you could have me to yourself. That's what monsters do first: They isolate people. And you prefer it when your prey doesn't seem to fight back, because then you can convince yourself that you're not a monster."

Again, Elias found himself taken aback by the boldness of her words. He disliked being spoken to in such a way. Elias felt his face beginning to distort with contempt, a movement that pulled his upper lip into a sneer.

She stepped from behind the cabinet. Elias flinched as he found her standing suddenly over him—a small woman, but heightened by confidence. Once again he was struck by her seeming familiarity, yet he couldn't place her. His gaze swept over her brown skin and badly cut hair, over the hideous pastel green jacket she wore.

Elias made a show of slowly getting to his feet. "How humbling," he said. "And how very smart of you."

"Is it smart of me?"

Elias moved closer, so that the two of them stood mere

inches apart. He stood at least half a foot taller than the woman. Though he loomed over her, she didn't waver. For a moment, Elias supposed it was to his advantage that she wasn't afraid. Fear got in the way of seduction, and that was one of his greatest arts. It took very little effort: He needed only gaze into the eyes, speak in a soothing voice, and exude intimacy rather than violence. Already he felt the quiet magnetism growing between the two of them; it was a subtle energy, full of silent nuance and unspoken invitations, and it usually succeeded.

She didn't feel it. Elias was allowed to edge closer to her, but there was no sudden self-doubt, no dreamy look in the eye, no relaxed and vulnerable sinking into his arms. Instead, she scoffed and gave him a mildly disgusted look. "I would ask how you became this way," she said, "but I already know the answer."

Elias felt the sneer returning to his face. "Do you?" he asked, hearing the uncharacteristic anger in his own voice. "Let me show you how I became this way. Then you can tell me if you were right."

Once again, he lunged—this time at her neck, his mouth open and ready to bite.

It was a clumsy attempt. Somehow, Elias stumbled on the woman's foot and lost his balance. They struggled, and he managed to shove her against the couch; her legs were knocked out from under her, and as she lay there prone and vulnerable, he went again for her throat.

Again, he missed. Elias, infuriated at his sudden incompetence, bit into her hand instead. His fangs sank into the soft flesh between her thumb and forefinger.

"Ow," she said.

Elias glared into her eyes as blood spilled into this mouth. She tried to yank her hand away, but only succeeded in further tearing her flesh.

"Okay, stop," she said. "You got me already."

His jaw slackened, but Elias found himself unwilling to withdraw.

"Seriously, I'm going to need surgery on this hand. I think you severed a nerve." The woman sat up as Elias finally drew back. She turned her hand to examine it, watched as blood streamed down to her elbow and dripped onto the couch. Elias felt something almost like embarrassment at the sight of it. He usually didn't allow himself to get this angry, or this messy. He knelt on the couch beside her, awkwardly trying to wipe away the blood that had spilled down his chin. The struggle had left him breathless; he wasn't accustomed to that either. He rarely had to put much effort into anything at all.

"I . . . dislike . . . fighting," he said aloud, still wiping at his face. He wasn't sure why he said it. He supposed that mentioning a mere "dislike" made him sound annoyed rather than outraged.

"Then why are you doing it?" she asked, still staring at the wound on her hand. Elias didn't answer, so she raised her eyes to look at him. "Did that tire you out?" she asked. "You don't exactly have that 'every day at the gym' vibe. It's more of a 'I go for a short walk once a month' kind of look. You seem winded."

The strangeness of the woman's behavior left him speechless.

"Did it tire you?" she asked again. "Let's find out."
She lunged.

Moments later, Elias somehow found himself in her place: pinned on his back against the couch cushions, with the woman's left shin on his chest and the other straddling his legs. He struggled to topple her, to grab her, but even with her injured hand she managed to hold his arms down. Her piercing brown eyes stared into his.

"You can stop struggling," she said. "I'm not going to harm you."

6

Elias stopped, trying to keep from panting. He hated the feeling of being overpowered, hated the feelings of anxiety and helplessness that began to stir deep inside him, like some just-awakened memory—and he hated that she could see his helplessness. No one had been able to overpower him since he'd become a vampire.

"Don't worry," she said. "I will be extraordinarily gentle."

Still grasping his wrist, she placed her forearm across his forehead—presumably to keep him from biting her as she moved her face closer to his. The woman's scents filled his nose as she closed in on his neck. Elias froze; it suddenly dawned on him that she might also be a monster. He usually knew such things right away, by the scent if nothing else—but perhaps she was some new breed, or perhaps the human scent she bore was a false one.

He felt her breath on his neck, on the scar that had formed there some years ago, when Elias himself had been bitten and turned. "Is this one of the places you were wounded?" she asked.

Elias thrashed again, but she held him fast, and he quickly gave up. "What are you?" he asked.

"A friend. Do you really not remember me, Elias Göransson?" A cryptic smile spread across her lips. "Oh—it's Elias Hellström now, isn't it? How Gothic."

Bruno's heavy footfalls were approaching. Elias heard one door flung open, then another. He abhorred the thought of that brute finding him in such a vulnerable position. Desperately, Elias tried to think of some other way to throw the woman off. His body wasn't strong enough, and his seductive powers had failed him.

"Have you noticed that I'm not turning into a vampire?" she asked.

Elias had, in fact, noticed: He had bitten her, but nothing had changed. There was no writhing agony, no

7

growl of helpless defiance, no sudden scent of death, no vague sharpening of the canine teeth. "You *are* obsessed with killing me," she continued, still looking steadily into his eyes. "I think it's me you've been seeking all this time. Me you want to hurt. Or maybe it's not about hurting me; maybe you just want to show me your pain. Isn't that what you really want, when you're getting ready to sink your teeth into those women?"

"I don't know you," he said.

"You do. You *did*. Think of a tomboy who likes music so much that she rarely ever takes off her headphones, and who often has her nose stuck in a book, and who's good at wrestling. No boy in the neighborhood has ever beaten me."

Abruptly, she leapt from the couch and stood in the middle of the room. By the time the door opened, she was standing in a strange manner, with her head hanging low and her shoulders slumped, looking weak and disconcerted.

Bruno rushed into the room and stopped in confusion, staring at the woman's hunched figure. With a slight movement he drew his face closer to her. Elias heard him sniff a couple of times, uselessly; Bruno's sense of smell was at its weakest during the new moon.

He only stood there for a moment before the woman's head jerked up. She hissed at Bruno and rushed past him.

Elias heard the slamming of her feet as she sprinted down the long hall. Bruno watched her go, and then regarded Elias with a puzzled expression. "What the hell was that?" His gaze fell to the blood-spattered cushions. "You bit her. Did she turn?"

Elias didn't like to admit bewilderment, but he stared down the hall in utter confusion and shook his head. "I have no idea what that was."

2

Even at his weakest, Bruno presented an intimidating figure. He was broad-shouldered and hulking, with a rugged face; his flat nose and square chin always made him look like he'd just been punched. His small eyes were a dull shade of blue, and his hair was styled in a crew cut that he rarely bothered to wash. In general, he was messy. His clothes were perpetually wrinkled, and he opted not to wash them (or himself) until his own odor made him wince with displeasure. His visits to the kitchen were visible in the smears, splatters, and crumbs he left behind, and Elias often found the bathroom sink coated with clippings from Bruno's occasional evening shave.

Elias, by contrast, required neatness. His room was immaculate, and his wardrobe carefully chosen. He loathed shorts and always wore dress pants or dark jeans, and preferred an open jacket over his shirt, simply because he thought it more stylish. Being a cold-blooded night creature allowed him to pull this off even in the warmer weather. He kept a collection of knit scarves for the winter months and purchased a couple of new wool coats every autumn. The night after the home intrusion was a particularly crisp fall night. When Elias came into the kitchen in a long gray coat and red scarf, Bruno complimented him on his new "ladies' coat" and "granny scarf."

"I wouldn't want to upstage you by dressing like an unwashed lumberjack," Elias replied, grabbing a thermos from the cupboard. "Remember to clean up after yourself, please."

"Where you going?" Bruno asked. "Leitha wants some study time before she goes out tonight. She's having trouble with JavaScript."

"I won't be gone long."

"At least come back before she goes clubbing. She'll want advice on that, too. Poor thing. She couldn't seduce a thirty-year-old virgin out of his mother's basement."

"She doesn't need to seduce anyone," Elias replied. "People are desperate. That's all it takes."

"Yes, but she's been settling for the old folks." Bruno sat down and peeled the rest of the plastic film from his microwave dinner, crumpling the sheet and tossing it onto the table. "Forty-year-olds, even older. You couldn't get me to go after that age group. There's hardly anything left to suck out of them." He forked up a bite of beef and macaroni, blowing on it before stuffing it into his mouth. "You can tell at a glance when people are past their prime," he said around his mouthful. "Once they get into their forties and fifties, they get kind of puffy and bloated, and their colors start to wash out—especially the lighter-skinned people. Their lips get pale, and their faces have kind of a gray, pasty undertone, like a bad potato."

"Yes, Bruno, I am aware of the 'potato phase' phenomenon," Elias replied. "I'm also the one who coined that phrase and described it to you last week. But thank you for making the effort to explain it back to me. You never know when I didn't understand what I was saying."

Bruno sneered as Elias brushed past him. "I'm just agreeing with you. Snarky little prick."

The Woodlands complex was situated in a secluded enough area, but it was only a few blocks from downtown—a mere six blocks to Main Street. That thoroughfare was populated with charming little shops

10

and a number of Gothic-style buildings, including the churches, city offices, and a small art museum. Elias didn't frequent the shops; he didn't want to become known. Tonight, though, he stopped at the closest coffee shop a few minutes before closing and sated his thirst with a thermos full of hot coffee and cream. This would not be a hunting night, at least not in the usual sense.

In the coffee joint he moved discreetly, keeping his head down and avoiding too much eye contact. That was what did it for the majority of his prey: locking gazes with him. A few moments of lingering eye contact and a sudden smile, and they were his.

With coffee in hand, Elias continued south along the main road until the busy shops gave way to a short stretch of woods. He kept going, stepping from sidewalk onto leaf-cluttered grass, past the trees and back to the place where he had subdued his last victim.

Achiravati Abbey was a monastery for bhikshunis, Buddhist nuns. To Elias, it was one of the ugliest places on the block. A circular drive and a large stone courtyard took up the foreground, with a puny fiberglass statue of the Buddha at the far edge. Behind that, a plaza of stone steps led up to a couple of large cabins, light tan-colored buildings with red trim. One, Elias knew, housed the few nuns who lived there; the other was for special events, or prayer, or whatever Buddhists did when they got together.

Elias had only entered the grounds once. He had stalked at this place. Preying so close to home, he knew, was a grave mistake—but he happened upon a woman coming alone from the monastery, and something about her drew him in. She was unremarkable, with a drooping face and short black hair that hung over her eyes, and a tight jacket that looked ready to burst its zipper. There was no happy, presumptuous smile, no innocent shine in her eyes, no glint of arrogance that he wanted to put to the test. It was her smell—something about it had triggered an intense thirst in him.

It wasn't until after the home intrusion that Elias noticed the similarity between her scent and that of the intruder: a smell of incense smoke blended with the heaviness of diffused oil, and even the more basic scent that reeked of late-teen or early-twenties hormones.

Elias had approached the droopy-faced woman with a friendly question about the monastery. They began to walk together toward town, past the stretch of trees, commenting on the sudden brisk weather, delving into mundane chatter. Before they reached the busy little shops and churches, Elias put an arm around her waist and drew her into the woods.

He was surprised by how little she struggled. Most of them didn't, but this woman was not his usual prey, and Elias hadn't really bothered to seduce her. She was stunned, it seemed, when he sank his teeth into her throat. The young woman tensed, and her heart raced, but several seconds passed before she lifted a hand in protest—a feeble effort to push Elias's face away. Then, rather calmly, she asked: "What the hell are you doing?"

Elias restrained the urge to laugh. He kept his mouth fixed in place as the woman's blood flowed into him, kept the effort clean and careful.

Preying on a human brought with it a certain set of thoughts and feelings. It started with a vacant sort of contempt: *You are nothing but my food.* As the blood began to fill his belly, it seemed to coat his feelings and sink them into oblivion. Elias always finished the task with indifference. A physical hunger had been sated; the act had no further significance.

The young woman kept her hand there, pressed against his face, as he drank. Before she fainted, she suddenly scratched him. He went home that night with a bleeding face, three scratches below his left eye, a smaller one from the nail of her little finger just above. They healed before morning.

Elias didn't wait to see if she turned. He never waited. As soon as she went limp, he lowered her to the ground and left her behind. He walked home in the usual state: full belly, empty mind. Feeding on a human always did that to him. For the rest of the night he would remain in a near zombie-like trance, incapable of feeling and thought—or perhaps not incapable, but unwilling.

Not all of his prey turned into vampires. A couple of times Elias had seen them later on, still human and very weak. He had fled from those areas, though the women didn't seem to remember him, and there was really no crime to pin on him. There had been no real struggle, never any attack—only a "consensual bite," Elias liked to think. Most of them didn't even question his advances, or offer the least bit of resistance. They just kept quiet and bled.

Elias didn't know why, but he had always attributed the phenomenon of "not turning" to weakness. He appreciated it, though. The fewer vampires, the better.

The stretch of trees came to an end, and Elias stood before the stone court, looking across the empty grounds at the two cabins that comprised the monastery. Even from a distance, he caught a familiar whiff of incense. Elias stood for some time and ruminated on the intruder's words: *My friend is dead because of you.*

The memory filled him with unease. He was shaken not only by her knowing his name, but by the fact that she seemed wholly unaffected by his bite. Supposedly, she was someone from his past. A tomboy who liked music and books, a skilled wrestler . . . .

As soon as he began to scroll through his memories, Elias' mind went blank. It was an automatic reaction. He disliked his past.

"The monastery is closed now," a voice said behind him, "but you can walk around the courtyard if you want."

Elias turned. A woman had come up behind him, presumably from the parking lot—an older woman, likely in her seventies, silver-haired with warm blue eyes and a friendly smile.

"Some people find it calming just to walk around the court," she said. "We discourage people from going up to the buildings at night, though."

"Thank you," Elias replied. "I just stopped to look. It's a beautiful place." He tried to veil his sarcasm; Elias found the grounds sloppily arranged and generally hideous.

He looked toward the buildings again, scanning the area for any sign of his intruder. It was irrational, he realized, to think that he would find her here. Perhaps another day, if he arrived in the morning instead of the eve, and if he was allowed to enter the monastery, they might have a chance encounter.

And if not, she would likely seek him out again. Whatever she wanted from Elias, she hadn't gotten yet.

At home, Leitha waited for him in the kitchen. It was the usual meeting place, being the only common area aside from the women's and men's bathrooms. There was also a TV lounge in the adjacent room, but only Bruno made use of it (and subsequently the room was filthy, aside from the times when Elias cleaned up the spilled food and discarded napkins, lest they attract more pests).

Leitha sat at the table with an empty cup of ramen. She had clearly been waiting for Elias; he found her slumped back against her chair, feet splayed, but she sat up straight when she saw him come in. "Vlad!" she said.

"Not my name," Elias replied.

"You said you were going to help with my coding."

"Yes, on Monday. You said you were going out tonight."

She got to her feet, looking up at him with an eager smile. "Help me with going out, then. What do you think of my outfit?" She half-turned, still casting him a flirtatious look. She was dressed in her typical fashion: a loose, glittery crop top over a very visible lace bra, and thong underwear that had crept up past the waist of her faded jeans. Elias had cut her hair so that it was close-cropped on the bottom, with a pile of tight curls on top. Leitha wore it well. She had a plumpness that flattered her; her full cheeks had a healthy glow, and in general she had a warm and inviting look about her. Unlike Elias, she exuded life. It was unfortunate, he thought, that she dressed like a twelve-year-old trying to pass as an adult.

"You'll need a coat," he replied. "It's cold out."

"I don't need one. I'm *hot*." Leitha's smile widened, and she gazed at Elias with unabashed interest. If Bruno had been present, he would have used the scene as ammunition against him. Bruno liked to say that Elias attracted girls because he was "pretty." The vampire had a pale, red-lipped face with long eyelashes, and he wore his white-blond hair in a cut that fell to his shoulders. His figure was slight but tall, and Leitha could often be found staring up at him with a silly grin on her face. The problem with Leitha was that she didn't know when to let up. It was a defining characteristic of the succubus.

"Don't overdo the smiling," Elias suggested. "It makes you look pathetic."

"It does not," she said. "It makes me look fun."

"And lose the thong underwear. I can practically see it crawling up your butt."

"What?" Leitha twisted around, trying to peer over her shoulder.

"The strap in the back is three inches above your pants," Elias said. "That's what happens when you've been wearing it for too long: the string gets pulled farther and farther in until it's chafing right into your porthole."

"It's supposed to be like that," she replied. "I want people to know I'm wearing it."

"It's unsanitary."

They debated the pluses and minuses of thongs for a few minutes, and then Leitha gave him one last adoring smile and headed for the doors. "Off to find my prey. Wish it was you, love."

"Because you're naive," Elias replied.

He retreated toward his rooms on the west end of the building. The complex was arranged so that each occupant had claim to one of the four corners of the building and the adjacent rooms. The rooms that belonged to Elias were mostly unfinished; he needed little more than his bedroom and his office, though he sometimes considered installing a kitchenette in one of the empty spaces, for the days when he didn't feel like cleaning up after Bruno. The corner room with the couch and empty file cabinets was one of his. The bedroom was adjacent to that, and beside it was the space where Elias performed fact checks and editing tasks for a fitness magazine, and some freelance work on the side.

Elias passed the TV lounge, where Bruno was lazing on one of the couches, reading comic books and listening to the *Blue Hawaii* soundtrack at a loud volume. Elias suppressed a sigh as he poked his head through the open doorway. Bruno's disregard for the house rules often got on his nerves, and the werewolf had plenty of opportunity to break them. Bruno spoke Russian, German, and Arabic, and was paid highly for his work as a translator, which meant that he had to work little more than three or four hours a night—and because he only went on the hunt

16

during the full moon, he most often stayed at home, finding countless ways to make noise, messes, and other annoyances. Elias often came into the TV lounge to find smears and crumbs scattered across the couch, with one clean spot in the shape of Bruno's hulking body.

"We have a rule about not blasting music in the common rooms," Elias shouted.

Bruno yelled back: "What common room? No one uses this room but me."

"At least shut the door, then." Elias closed the door and kept walking, but stopped at the next room—one that technically belonged to him. In the past, it had served as a health lab. The room still contained a number of abandoned supplies: centrifuges, test kits, urine cups, boxes full of specimen tubes.

Elias stepped into the room and flicked on the light. To his left was a cabinet with a pair of file drawers at the bottom. He scanned the room, looking at the dust-coated boxes and gadgets, and knelt to open one of the drawers. The first folder was full of blank requisition forms, while the others contained directions for the proper collection and storage of specimens. Elias pulled a sheet from the folder labeled "Hepatitis C" and read through it, noting the directions on the storage protocol and the procedures for separating plasma from blood.

Ever since meeting the strange intruder, a question had nagged at him: After being bitten by a vampire, why didn't everyone turn? True, Elias had bitten the intruder for less than a minute, but her blood should have been affected. And she wasn't the only one; there had been two others, at least, who endured his bite without becoming vampires themselves. Elias had begun to wonder if some quality of the blood made them immune. Perhaps the weakness was in his own blood.

The subject had never interested him before, but the

intruder had sparked a practical curiosity in him. Would others react to his bite the same way? So far, his prey had presented little threat. The ones who became vampires took to the night hours, keeping quiet, avoiding friends and family. Victor sometimes saw them at night, creeping in the shadows. If they remembered him, they didn't acknowledge it. They avoided him as though they were repelled—and there weren't many of them, but Elias sometimes wondered how large a chain he had created, how many of his vampires had created other vampires, how often they fed. His own need for blood was unpredictable, but he could usually go for weeks without feeding. His longest fast from blood had lasted nearly six full moons.

Not all vampires were so reserved. Another vampire had lived in the complex before Leitha: Viktor, a young, careless, and perpetually thirsty creature. He had died a particularly gruesome death, making headlines in a neighboring town when pieces of his body turned up in a major river, each part wrapped in a plastic trash bag. Elias still feared that it had been a revenge killing—that someone knew what Viktor was, perhaps even knew where he lived. Viktor's carelessness could have drawn attention to the office complex and the other monsters living in it. Elias had no desire to flee again. He enjoyed his current living arrangement, though his roommates were far from ideal.

Elias read through the direction sheet again and turned to look at the boxes of specimen tubes. He searched until he found the tubes that matched the instruction sheet and pulled out a single vial, examining it thoughtfully.

It was possible, he supposed, to examine his own blood in this laboratory. He could easily obtain samples from a few humans, and with some careful study, he could compare the samples to see how his own blood had changed. It would give him something to do besides work, wander, and hunt. Vampires, in general, were a boring lot, without hobbies or friends to occupy their time.

Unbeknownst to Elias, he was taking an initial step toward self-reflection. It was the first time he questioned why he had become a vampire.

3

The sun hadn't yet risen above the horizon, but it had already streaked the sky with yellow, pink, and purple hues. Elias stood at the window of the coffee shop, looking in at the faces illuminated by the overhead lights. He didn't recognize any of the workers or customers. He assured himself that the morning crowd was surely a different group than the night crowd, and would not recognize him or try to make friendly advances. The vampire stepped inside, thermos in hand. He asked the woman at the counter to fill it for him, making minimal eye contact as she replied with "Sure, honey" and "There you go, hon."

Elias had no particular goal in mind as he wandered the early morning streets. He had already cleaned and organized the lab, and had even run some tests on his own blood. More research was required to determine the meaning of those results. In the meantime, as Elias wandered, he pondered how to get a sample from a human. He could do it the next time he fed—but how to do it cleanly, and without invoking the wrath of the intruder?

He stood on a street corner, looking in the direction of the monastery and ruminating on the intruder's warning: *If you ever try to do that to anyone again, I will take back every drop of blood you've stolen . . . .*

"Unlikely," he murmured.

A familiar voice spoke up behind him: "Looking for someone?"

Elias turned toward the sound, and there she was: the woman with the ugly haircut and hideous pastel jacket. She stood downwind; otherwise he would have surely caught her scent, and she would not have caught him off guard.

Elias tensed and took a step back.

"What's the matter?" the woman asked. She stood with her hands in her jacket pockets, shoulders hunched against the cold. "Afraid I'm going to pin you again? I suppose you hate being shown up by a girl—just like all the other boys I grew up with."

Elias looked around at the semi-busy street. People all along the block were walking dogs, stepping in and out of stores, and passing by in cars, and the morning was getting lighter and lighter. In a low voice, Elias asked: "What is it that you want? Revenge for your friend?"

The woman gave him a sad smile. "Never mind what I want. With people like you, I can't afford to be predictable."

"I see. Is that why you burst into my house? You were trying to be unpredictable?"

"You call that place a house?"

She stepped closer. Elias moved back, but she simply walked past him, going at a casual pace around the corner and onto the side street.

Elias stood there, perplexed, and then went after her. He stayed a few paces behind, still trying to speak in a quiet tone. "So, what, then? Are you just going to randomly pop up and make threats, or trespass in my home? I wouldn't recommend doing that again, by the way. You were lucky that time."

She turned her head, calling back to him: "How so?"

"The . . . ." Elias hesitated. "The worst of us wasn't at home. That might not be the case next time."

"Are you concerned for me?"

21

"Should I be? I don't know who you are."

The woman turned toward him, walking backwards a few paces as she spoke. Elias looked into her large brown eyes and felt a pang of recognition, but her identity eluded him. "I'll give you another hint," she said. "When I left, I promised I would come back for you." She turned away, adding: "And here I am."

Once again, memories of the past began to stir—but a strange, subtle pain seemed to course through Elias' mind, and the recollections ceased.

"Do you know what's down this street?" she asked.

"I do," he replied. "A liquor store, an empty office building, and a sad cemetery."

"What's sad about it?"

"On Memorial Day," he replied, "and on every other day, there are never any flowers or pretty little things on the graves. The lawn is overgrown, there's litter everywhere, and there's a crumbling fountain in the middle that never has any water in it."

Elias maintained a cool manner as he trailed after the woman. He was keenly aware that the woman was leading him, and he knew not where—but he needed to find out who she was and what she wanted from him. With caution, Elias tried once again to delve into his memories. He saw flashes of those brown eyes, heard echoes of the woman's voice—or a voice remarkably like hers—but he still couldn't remember.

The path into the cemetery was flanked by two stone pillars and iron gates that never closed. The woman walked inside, and Elias followed her down the left-hand path. As they walked between headstones and monuments, the vampire cast an anxious glance at the sky. The sun was rising. Elias could see the headstones becoming more defined in the morning light, could read the labels on the candy wrappers strewn across the leaf-cluttered ground, and the sight made him wince. It wasn't really the light itself that bothered him, but its revelatory quality. He hated the day because he didn't want to be seen.

The woman stopped in front of a wide columbarium. It was wide enough to hold more than a hundred urns on the front-facing side, in columns of six. The woman stood at at the last column and studied one of the memorial plaques.

"Why did you go to the abbey?" she asked, without looking at him.

Still keeping his cool, Elias replied: "I was intrigued by its ugliness. I thought Buddhists were supposed to know about cosmic order and feng shui and such things, but whoever designed that place has no concept of aesthetic beauty. It's no wonder it got booted to the outskirts of town."

"You killed my friend at that ugly abbey. Her name was Zoua. But I suppose you never knew her name."

Elias' eyes drifted to the name on the plaque: Zoua Vang. The inscription was a simple one, bearing only her name and the dates of her birth and death. "I suppose not," he said. "But I know I've never killed anyone."

"What made you go after her?"

Elias hesitated.

"She was wearing my clothes," the woman said, turning to look at him. She waited for her meaning to sink in, and added: "We did a Medicine Buddha puja at the abbey that night. Zoua had to walk home afterward, and it was cold out, so I let her borrow my jacket. Why did you go after her?"

A slow realization began to sink in. He had gone after that woman because of her smell. No—because of the way the jacket smelled. As Elias stood looking into this woman's face, breathing her familiar scent, he realized that he must know her—that he had, unconsciously, been seeking her that night.

"I have a thing for nuns," he replied lamely, not wanting to show his unease.

"She wasn't a nun. Zoua was in prison until a few months ago. She was in the abbey's prison outreach program. After she was released, she started volunteering at the monastery. She was about to start a residency there."

Elias tried to bring the conversation back to the woman's identity. "And what about you? You're a nun?"

"I'm a volunteer. I go there to cook, clean, stuff envelopes, do a little gardening. Have fun with friends." She stood with her arms folded over her chest, staring at him with her penetrating brown eyes. Elias noticed for the first time the bandage around her right hand, a strip of gauze wrapped around the place where he had bitten her. "I wonder why you chose a monastery to hunt your prey," she said. "Why you *really* chose it. Did you like the idea of hunting something associated with prayer and holiness? Or was Zoua just another meal?"

He didn't answer, so she continued: "She called me that night when she got home. She told me she was turning into a vampire. She was trying to fight it off, but she knew she wasn't going to win."

"Really. She told you she was becoming a vampire, and you just believed her?"

"I've been bitten before," the woman replied. "I know all about vampires and other monsters. I've met them."

"Really," Elias said again.

"Zoua wanted me to kill her. She begged me to cut off her head, or to drive a stake through her heart."

"So *you* killed her," Elias said.

"Of course not. I said I would bring her to the monastery, so we could pray with her."

"And?"

"And she killed herself before I could get there." The woman's voice broke as she said the words, and Elias saw the sudden welling of tears in her eyes. "But I would have gone for the stake, if I didn't know any better. Do you know why vampires die when you destroy their hearts?"

Elias tried to think of a clever response, and failed.

"Vampires are looking for something to sate their hearts," she answered for him. Elias saw that she was struggling to speak through her grief. "They think they can get it by draining other people's hearts, but they can never find it by feeding. When you destroy a vampire's heart, there is nothing left to sate, and so they have to give up."

"How poetic," Elias replied dryly. "And why do they die when you decapitate them?"

"I suppose they die for convenience's sake. Who wants to live forever without a head?"

She walked on. Elias watched her retreat down the path, and then he followed again, hurrying to walk beside her. "So you blame me for your friend's death," he said when he had caught up with her, "but you also said that you're not going to harm me—unless I attack someone else. Is that right?"

"That's right," she replied.

"Then, what is it that you want?"

"I want to destroy a vampire."

Elias studied her face, saw grief still etched in her features. The woman was looking at the ground as she walked, or at the trees and stones ahead of them—anywhere but him. "Which one?" he asked. "The one who bit you before?"

Strangely, she smiled. "No."

"Why do you think your friend became a vampire, and you didn't?"

"Zoua didn't feel worthy of prayer and help," the woman said. "She always struggled with that. She had done too many things that she was ashamed of. I think that's what does it: when the idea of staying human is too painful, and the idea of defeating monsters seems impossible."

"How philosophical. And what about you?"

She shrugged. "Maybe I've just learned enough to know better."

"Oh, so you skipped right into the crone phase," Elias replied. "People much older than you have turned. You can't be more than twenty."

"Older in years, maybe, but not in experience. If your soul hasn't evolved enough to have conquered jealousy, insecurity, and other types of pettiness, then it's more prone."

"So think of yourself as more evolved than other people."

"It isn't a brag. I've been tested a lot."

They had looped through the middle of the cemetery and were circling back toward the gates. Elias encouraged the woman to keep talking, hoping to get another clue as to what she was after. "Do you believe in reincarnation, then?" he asked. "Aging and evolving through multiple lives?"

She shrugged. "I don't remember any past lives. Maybe I've lived before, maybe I haven't." She looked up at him, finally, with a steady gaze. "But I've lived enough, and been tested enough, and lived vicariously through others enough to know how to avoid becoming a vampire. I've even learned from you, Elias. I know why you became a vampire—why you felt like defeating monsters is impossible, and why you must have been terrified of staying human."

Elias stopped walking, startled by the audacity of her

words. No, not startled, but angry. The woman's claim had struck some deep, forgotten nerve in him, a raw and fragile nerve that was better left untouched.

"Do you still not recognize me?" she asked, facing him. "You know me from a past that you would rather not remember. Isn't that right? What happened in your past that was so awful, you blocked it all out?" Her gaze intensified, her eyes seeming to glow with the effort to make him remember. "Think of a green sign that says 'Pine Knoll,' and imagine a girl who looks like me, except she's at least six years younger, with long hair. She's sitting on a gray rock at the end of a wooden bridge, and waiting for you, and when you get there she hands you her headphones and says that you have to listen. Think about walking with her on dirt trails in the woods, climbing the bluffs with her and building little forts at the top, and taking a raft through the swamp—and at dinner time you would have to go back home, to a man who was a monster to you. And even though you had to live with him, you still had a friend who loved you." Again, the woman's voice faltered with some deep emotion. "Someone who gave you music to help you feel better," she continued, "and stories to take your mind off of your problems. Who was that friend for you?"

And then the memories raced in, so fast that Elias couldn't stop them: a girl with brown eyes and a lively smile, a tough tomboy with long, dark hair pulled back into a messy braid, a girl who threatened boys and raised her fists, a girl with headphones pressed into the mane of her hair—and a darker vision of a man towering over him, a man whose face he couldn't quite remember, but whose actions came back to Elias in a repulsive flood of memory. Elias tried to stop the flow, but it was too late: some barrier between the present and past had been broken, and that past was no longer hidden, but blazing in the full light of day.

"Aarya," he said. "Aarya Khurana."

She looked at him without speaking. Elias prodded her: "Is it you?"

"It is," she replied softly.

A mixture of feelings coursed through him, all of which he suppressed. In a controlled voice, Elias asked: "What the hell did you do to your hair?"

Aarya raised a hand, gingerly touching the back of her head. "I cut it."

He tried to think of some other snide, indifferent quip, but found himself at a loss. His thoughts were drowned in a growing tumult of anger and disgust, even a strain of deep despair.

Abruptly, he started away.

"Elias," she called after him.

He heard the sound of dry leaves crunching under her feet as she hurried to catch up. "Why are you running from me?"

"You're from my past," he replied bitterly, and quickened his pace. "Stay there."

"I'm in your present. I have been, this whole time." Aarya's footsteps still sounded behind him, slowing their pace. "Remember, you know where to find me," she called.

Elias passed between the stone columns and out of the cemetery. He turned right at the sidewalk, heading back toward home. He was certain he heard Aarya's steps on the pavement, but when he glanced back, she wasn't there.

The sight of the empty walkway struck him with a strange sense of regret. Elias shook it off and kept walking. Regret, grief, longing—those were things that he was unwilling to waste his time on. *Not anymore*, he thought to himself. *Never again.*

4

Elias spent the day sleeping. Such was his usual routine. In the evening, though, he stayed in bed later than usual. Getting up and facing another night seemed suddenly off-putting: the same work, the same boredom, the same wandering. And now the banality would be washed in the ugly residue of his now-remembered past.

He found himself surprised, though, after he finally got up and dressed himself. As Elias approached the front of the building, he smelled coffee brewing in the kitchen. Bruno's coffee, by the scent of it. The werewolf wasn't a great cook, but his coffee was divine. He was making pancakes, too—Elias could smell the batter—but those were nothing to get excited about. Bruno always made them too thick, burnt on the outside and raw in the middle.

Elias went to the kitchen and headed straight for the coffee mugs. "Good morning, Bruno. Did you make a full pot?"

"I did," Bruno replied. He stood near the stove, cracking an egg into a mixing bowl. "Help yourself."

"Thanks." Elias poured himself a cup and opened the fridge. "Where's the cream?"

"Gone. We were out of milk, so I used it for the pancakes."

"Fine." Elias closed the refrigerator. "I'll forgive it, since . . . ." He trailed off as he turned toward the kitchen table. A boy was sitting there, facing him. A young boy, perhaps three or four years old, with wide eyes and a messy bowl cut. An empty plate and fork were set before him, along with a plastic juice cup. He stared at Elias wordlessly.

Elias asked: "Why is there a child sitting at our table?"

"He's mine," Bruno replied.

"In what way?"

"He's my son, genius. I do have other cravings besides raw meat and brew. I had a fling with his mother a few years back."

The boy picked up the juice cup and drank, staring at Elias over the rim. Elias locked gazes with him and felt a creeping sense of dread. "Why is he here?"

The wooden spoon clattered against the sides of the mixing bowl. Bruno spoke over the noise: "He's my flesh and blood, isn't he? I'm going to make sure he grows up proper. Rather be the hunter rather than the prey, and all that."

Elias' dread crept up into his throat. "Where is his mother?" he asked.

A sizzling sound erupted from the pan as batter collided with oil. "Do I detect a note of concern?" Bruno asked. "Have you developed a soft spot for kids, or are you just hard up for reasons to look down your nose at everyone? Oh, save the children; we need them to get to a ripe age so we can ravage them. Is that it?"

The coffee seemed to curdle in Elias' stomach. He emptied his mug in the sink and set it in the dishwasher. "Please quit with the monster talk. Today, it disgusts me."

"Why'd you pour it, if you weren't going to drink it?" Bruno asked. "And never mind where his mother is. Take my word for it: there won't be any interference from her."

"I see. And who's going to raise him?"

"Don't worry, I won't try to shove him off on you. I'm handling him, aren't I?"

Elias stopped in the entryway and turned to stare at

him. He spoke in a cold tone. "Have you done something that's going to get us into trouble?"

The werewolf scoffed. "I've done plenty, you overgrown leech. So have you. You think all of your chomping on girls' throats isn't going to get us all into trouble some day?"

Elias left the kitchen. He was halfway down the hall when he stopped, suddenly aware that he was having trouble breathing. Some strange sensation had filled his lungs, like a veil of mist had settled inside them. Elias placed a hand to his chest and took a slow breath.

Leitha came around the corner. She started to smile, and then looked at Elias with concern. "What's the matter?"

"Nothing," he said. "I just felt weird for a second . . . like I couldn't breathe."

"When you saw me, right?" she asked, grinning and batting her eyes. "It happens to a lot of guys. Are you going to help me with coding?"

"Sure."

They retreated back to her office, and Leitha pulled up the page she was working on. "It's this," she said, pointing to an editing box full of type. "I'm having trouble writing functions. They don't work out."

Elias peered at the screen. "It's because you're overdoing it. You have too many parameters, and your coding is a mess. Here." He leaned over beside her, deleting most of her text. "You probably had it right when you started out. Just practice making functions with one or two variables until you get the hang of it."

She was looking up at him with stifling affection, a wide smile plastered on her face. "Vlad," she said.

"Not my name," he replied curtly.

She swiveled gently back and forth in the chair. "You like me, right?"

"I don't resent you as much as I resent the others."

"You like me," she repeated, letting her head fall coyly against her shoulder. "And you have a lovely leather sofa in your office that's the perfect size for both of us—well, the perfect size if we're sort of stacked, with you on your back and me roving around on top. It's quieter than a bed."

"Not gonna happen, Leitha."

"Afraid I'm going to drain you?" she asked. "You know I couldn't. Not you."

"It's not about that. I don't dislike you, but I think of you as a little sister."

The smile wavered. A momentary look of hurt flashed in Leitha's eyes. "Right," she said. "I'm everyone's little sister, aren't I? Not a real woman, but just a silly little thing to be lectured and laughed at."

"Don't accuse me of lecturing you," Elias replied. "You ask for my advice."

"But it's not your advice that I want."

Elias sighed. "I have to get started on my own work. Keep practicing with this, okay?"

He went out before she could protest, closing the door behind him and headed back to his own office. Elias was beginning to detest his "help" sessions with Leitha, no matter how brief—but the Woodlands complex was not cheap, and Leitha wasn't pulling her weight with the rent. She needed another skill set, one that didn't primarily depend on luring older men and extorting from them their valuables and their finances. Web development was something she was capable of, and that she could do remotely, during the night hours.

Elias had trouble performing his own editing tasks that night. He was distracted, and ended up reviewing his work several times before submitting it. Elias rarely ever made mistakes in his work, simply because he couldn't afford to. On top of his own expenses, he sometimes had to cover a share of rent for the others, and he maintained a hefty savings account in case one of his roommates decided to leave—or in case they ended up like Viktor.

He gave up working and focused instead on cleaning the bathrooms and the kitchen. Morning hadn't yet arrived by the time he finished. Elias went back to the lab and pulled out a text he'd been reading on genetic trends. He flipped through pages, highlighting and making notes in the margins, and then switched on one of the computers and perused the software programs. He'd started his research with several shots in the dark, focusing on genetic traits associated with disease and deviant behavior, and already he'd found some interesting results in his own blood work: a key dopamine receptor carried an A1 allele, one that indicated susceptibility to unhealthy cravings. It would be interesting, he thought, to get a sample of the mystery intruder's blood for comparison. Perhaps she simply wasn't coded to thirst after the blood of others.

Dawn approached, but Elias knew he wouldn't sleep any time soon. The addition of a human child to the household, and Leitha's sullen accusations, had done nothing to distract him from the constant nagging of his memories. It was no use trying to forget. Aarya had cracked his past wide open; Elias could no longer wall it up and pretend not to know. Nor could he stop trying to figure out what exactly it was that Aarya wanted from him. When he'd asked, she had given a cryptic answer: *I want to destroy a vampire.* Was she trying to destroy him, then, by leading him into some disaster? Or did she think she could destroy the vampire part of him, and bring back the boy she'd known in her childhood—a boy who no longer existed?

Before sunrise Elias trekked out to the monastery, and

33

although the windows lit up around five o'clock, the grounds remained empty. Elias turned toward home, taking the route past the cemetery. That, too, was deserted. He walked back to the Woodlands complex and hesitated in the lot. Sunrise was still more than half an hour away. He had just enough time to try one more place. Aarya had said he would know where to find her, so Elias got into his car and drove to the place she had described: a neighborhood with a green sign that read "Pine Knoll." In the middle of that neighborhood was a wooden bridge leading over a marshland, now dry and choked with weeds. Elias parked on the road near the foot bridge. An old Chevy was also parked there, a deep red car with a line of rust along the bottom.

As Elias walked across the bridge, he saw the gray boulder on the opposite side, and on top of it was a splash of color: a hideous shade of pastel green, and the dark blue of Aarya's jeans. She was lying on her side, listening to music on an MP3 player. When Elias reached the rock, Aarya pulled the ear buds out and extended them to him. "Do you want to listen?"

"No."

She sat up. She looked tired, with a hint of dark circles under her eyes, and her short hair looked stiff and disheveled.

"Have you been lying on this rock since yesterday?" he asked.

"I haven't been here long. But I came last night, too, just in case." Aarya pocketed the ear buds and slid off of the rock. "Remember these trails?" she asked, pointing to a fork in the dirt path. "They're still the same. We can take the bluff trail. Just like old times."

"If you want," Elias replied.

They began to walk, and Elias started right away with his questions. "How did you know it was me who bit your friend?" he asked. "I mean, how did you know it was *me*. Did you see me, and recognize me?"

"You know how people say that killers return to the scene of the crime, for whatever reason? Maybe they want to re-live the experience. Or maybe, in your case, you just wanted to know what drew you there in the first place. What did draw you there? You never answered me."

"Chance," Elias replied. "I'm not a killer, and you didn't answer my question either. How did you know it was me?"

"You came back to the abbey. I saw a strange man standing there and staring at the buildings, so I followed him. That's how I figured out where you lived. A private detective helped me with the rest. When I saw the name Elias listed at that address, I looked into it further, and I found out that you had changed your last name—to Hellström, of all things."

"You hired a private detective?" Elias asked sharply. "And you told this person that I attacked your friend?"

"I said that I was investigating a suspicious person who had been hanging around the abbey. She didn't ask a lot of questions; she just wanted money for the job. Anyway, she's not investigating anymore. When I realized it was you, I took over."

"What do you mean? You're investigating?"

"I've been watching," Aarya replied.

"Oh, you watched. And that made you confident about walking into my home and potentially taking on a pack of murderous beasts."

"Not particularly. But I went in anyway."

"Why?"

"For you." Aarya glanced at him, and Elias winced under her gaze. "I needed to see how you were living."

"Why?" he asked again, wondering what she had seen.

"For a lot of reasons. I needed to know how much of a monster you'd become. And I wanted to know . . . ."

Elias stopped walking. "Yes, I'm a monster, if that's what you like to call it," he said. "And my life is damned good as a so-called monster. It's the *only* time my life has been any good."

"Wasn't it good with me?" she asked, turning to face him.

"Oh, yes, because you're so evolved. You think you're the cream of everyone's crop, don't you?"

"That's not what I mean, Elias. I meant that the two of us—"

"Don't act like the two of us had any kind of power together," he snapped. "Yes, you talked to me, you gave me CDs and we shared books, but it was no more than anyone else did. Other people talked, and other people gave things, but no one stepped up to help me with the one thing I actually needed. People knew what was happening to me."

Aarya's eyes exuded sympathy. Elias hated that look. "Yeah, some people suspected your stepfather," she said. "I know he hurt you. But—"

"He didn't just 'hurt' me," Elias said, his voice rising. "Hurt? He ruined everything about me that was human. I couldn't do anything I wanted to do with my life. I couldn't date, get married, have a family. I didn't want anyone touching me. I couldn't deal with the anxiety of raising a child. I hated people and I didn't want to be one of them. When I was bitten, that was the last straw. I decided to adjust to being a vampire. It was better than being part of humanity . . . a race of weak, delusional, spineless hypocrites."

She regarded him coolly. "Are you not a spineless hypocrite now?"

He raised a finger to her face, as if to scold her, but

the words didn't come.

"You hurt people," she said, "and leave them with nothing but pain."

"That's not the same. It's one bite, not years of abuse—and the pain is their own. Isn't that what you've been telling me: that it's our own pain, and our own weakness, that makes us turn into vampires? And of course that will never happen to you, because you're so mighty and good, and now you're going to teach me how to overcome my pain. Right?" Elias raised the pitch of his voice, mimicking: "'When I left, I promised I would come back for you, and here I am.' You came here by chance."

"I came back to this area for you," Aarya said. "When I turned eighteen—"

"Oh, how heroic of you. Even if you did, you came back when it's far too late! What good is it now? Does it make you feel better to say 'Oh, sorry about all that, I really wish I could've done something, but I was busy skiing and river rafting with my friends in Colorado,' or wherever the hell you went. It must be tempting to pat yourself on the back for showing up now, when you don't have to stick your neck out for anyone."

Aarya glanced up, alerted by the sound of crackling farther down the path—a squirrel or some other animal, probably. She and Elias were still alone, but she lowered her voice to a loud whisper, as if afraid of being overheard. "Why are you accusing me? I was a kid, too. I didn't have any power."

"Fine, but don't act like you're swooping back here to save me like some sort of superhero."

"It's not about being a hero," she said. "I'm just extending an invitation."

"To what?"

"To not being a vampire."

Elias scoffed. "And you know all about how to do that, do you? Even though you're so good that you've never become one?"

"I grew up like that, too," she said, with a sudden quavering in her voice. "For the two years that my mom's brother lived with us, I felt the same way. I have been just as angry, and helpless, and just as . . . sad."

"It was different with you," he replied.

"How so?"

"Your parents found out and moved you away from him."

"Bullshit, Elias, you know that's not how it happened. It went on for months, and yes, my parents finally moved me away. They moved me away from you and all of my friends, and everyone I loved, so they wouldn't have to face him and acknowledge what was happening. And you know what? After we left, he probably went after other girls, because no one ever bothered to hold him accountable."

Elias saw the genuine despair in Aarya's eyes. It quelled his anger; he no longer felt like accusing her. "I'm sorry," he said instead. Elias began to walk again, and Aarya kept pace beside him. "I'm not really angry that you had to leave," he added. "It's just . . . I had forgotten about everything, and you reminded me." He glanced at her. "I hate you for that."

"Did you really forget, though? I think it's what drives you to prey on other people. Maybe you don't think about it in detail, but you didn't forget—about him, or about me. I checked around to see if there were any other attacks like the one that happened to Zoua, and I found a couple of police reports about women being bitten. One happened at the park where we used to go Rollerblading, and the other one happened outside the arcade we used to go to. I actually went there and asked about it, and I met

38

the person you attacked. She works there. She's the same age as us, and we look a little bit alike—not that much, but she has the same hair color and the same eyes, and she's even Indian." She gave him a pointed look. "That was you, wasn't it?"

Elias lowered his eyes. Aarya took his silence as an affirmation.

"I brought you to those places," she said. "When you targeted those women, weren't you really going after me?"

Aarya waited for a response, but Elias stayed quiet and expressionless. "I really did come back here for you," she said. "Can you imagine how I felt when I found out that you were the one who bit Zoua? Her pain was enough, but you gave her yours, too. That's what happens when you bite people."

Elias suppressed the urge to say something defensive. Instead he asked: "Will you really drain my blood if I bite someone again?"

"I will," she replied. "It wasn't an empty threat."

"And how will you do it? With what?"

"Never mind how I'll do it. It's a surprise."

"Right. You don't want to be predictable."

She smiled a little. After a moment she pulled the ear buds out of her pocket. "Listen," she said, but Elias shooed her hand away.

"I don't listen to music anymore," he said.

"Fine."

Elias stopped again. They had reached the bluffs, the small rocky walls that they had climbed together as children. He gazed up at them as he spoke. "It's getting light," he said, "so I'm going to head back."

"All right."

Elias didn't start back, but looked at Aarya in silence for some time. "What happens next?" he asked.

39

"See me again," she replied. "Every morning, or every night. You pick."

Elias found that he disliked the idea of not seeing her again. He had a sudden need to look into the warmth of her eyes, to say something to make her smile. Even the bad haircut suddenly held a certain charm for him. "Tomorrow morning," he said.

"Don't stand me up," she replied.

Aarya walked him back to his car. She waved as he began to drive away, and as Elias turned and headed back down the street, he told himself that it was a good-bye wave. He would likely come back to find an empty rock, or a note from Aarya saying she had business in Colorado.

In spite of himself, Elias knew that she would be there. The knowledge gave him an unexpected sense of comfort.

5

After another day of sleep, Elias could hardly wait to pass the night. Once again he was distracted in his work. He began to wish that he had chosen night instead of day to meet Aarya—and he assured himself that he only wanted to see her because he was curious, because she presented an interruption to his otherwise mundane life.

He laundered and ironed his clothes, and then took a midnight break in the kitchen, drawn by the smell of Bruno's coffee. The little boy was at the table again, sitting on a thick training manual that Bruno had made into a booster seat, with a plate full of pancakes in front of him.

"Are you going to feed him anything else?" Elias asked as he pulled a mug from the cupboard.

"He likes pancakes," Bruno replied. "What's it to you?"

Elias watched as the boy tore a cake apart with his fingers, stuffing a too-large piece into his mouth. He tried to swallow, then coughed and tried to wash it down with juice.

Elias set his mug down and grabbed a butter knife from the drawer. "You have to cut it for him," he said, leaning over the table. He grabbed the child's fork and sliced the pancake into small squares.

"He's a kid," Bruno said. "He can eat with his fingers if he wants."

Elias forked a piece of pancake and handed it to the boy. "What's his name?"

"Luka," Bruno replied. "Not my choice. I would've picked a strong name, like Gunther. Or maybe Hans, after my brother."

"After your brother? I didn't take you for a sentimental person."

"I don't feel sentimental about him. He was the first person I killed."

Elias gave the werewolf an uneasy look. He forgot, sometimes, the things his roommates had done—the things they still did. In the ordinary routines of home life, it was easy to forget that he lived with murderers.

Elias, of course, liked to believe that he had never killed anyone.

Bruno stood up and headed through the entryway. Elias called after him: "Where are you going?"

"To take a piss," Bruno called back.

Elias poured his coffee and cream. He turned, standing with his back against the counter; he took a slow sip, and then another, while Luka sat and watched him.

Elias gave the boy a light scowl. "What are you looking at?"

Luka didn't reply, but kept his eyes fixed on Elias' face as he forked another bite of pancake into his mouth.

"Do you talk?" Elias asked. "Or do you just stare at people?"

The child continued to stare.

"Where is your mother?" Elias glanced toward the hallway, lowering his voice. "Your mom. Where is she?"

Luka chewed and swallowed. Then, in a soft voice, he said: "Mama."

"Right. Mama." Elias looked the boy over. Luka was difficult to read; he'd only had one expression thus far, one of watchful but semi-vacant silence. He didn't seem afraid, but he didn't act normal either. The boy was old enough to be able to speak more than a word or two.

Perhaps he had always been quiet, but Elias thought it more likely that the boy had been traumatized by the sudden, possibly violent interruption to his life. "Do you miss her?" Elias asked.

The child didn't respond, but just sat looking at him.

Elias sighed, a long exhale that hissed through clenched teeth. "Christ, you're young. What the hell is he thinking?"

"I heard that," Bruno said as he came back into the kitchen. "I'm thinking I don't want him to grow up to be a cream horn, that's what." He brushed past Elias and added: "Arrogant twat."

"What the hell is a cream horn?"

"A soft, delicious delicacy. Easy to bite into." Bruno reached out and ruffled Luka's hair. "This one's going to bite back."

Luka turned his head to look up at Bruno. He didn't speak, but stuffed the last bite of pancake into his mouth and chewed.

"It'll take time," Bruno said.

Elias looked at the boy again, searching for some glimmer of emotion in the boy's eyes—sadness, uncertainty, worry—but saw none. Luka stuffed his mouth and stared, first at Elias, then at Bruno.

Elias left the kitchen and finished his coffee in his office. He was hungry, he realized. He typically had a meager diet, and could satisfy himself with a snack at lunch time, but now he wanted a meal. The idea of spending time in the kitchen with Bruno repelled him, so Elias went to his car and drove to a midnight diner.

The place was small and poorly lit and reeked of vegetable oil. Elias remembered the menu being decent enough, but the more he looked through the options and the poorly done photos of heaping plates of food, the less appetizing it all seemed.

43

The waitress came back to his booth. "What can I get you?" she asked.

"I don't know," Elias replied. "I just want food."

She raised her eyebrows. "You just want food, huh? Do you need some suggestions?"

Elias glanced across the dining room. Another customer sat there, slowly picking away at a plate of eggs and toast. "I'll have eggs and toast," Elias said. "And a side of fruit."

"What kind of toast?"

Elias pointed. "Whatever he's having."

When the food arrived, the vampire took little pleasure in eating it. Even now, when he craved food, he disliked its texture in his mouth. The act of chewing, swallowing, and digesting always seemed tedious and crude, no less tonight than any other night. Nor did he enjoy the near-constant attention of the waitress, who had only the one other customer, and who kept stopping by Elias' table to pester him with questions and inane small talk. He hadn't even started on the eggs or fruit when she came to the table for the eighth time.

"Everything okay?" she asked.

Elias was staring at the plate. Wordlessly, he pulled a long, gray hair from the clump of scrambled eggs. It hung heavy in his hand, weighed down by bits of egg. He held it up for the waitress to see.

"Oh," she said. "I'm so sorry. I'll get you a new plate."

"Just the check, please." Elias looked at the woman's neck as he spoke. She wasn't the culprit whose hair had strayed into his food; she had light brown hair, swept into a bun that left the length of her neck exposed. Elias, still hungry and suddenly without a meal, found himself suddenly aware of the blood flowing beneath the woman's flesh. She would make an easy target; she was already

44

fawning over him, wanting to please him. A bite to a stranger's neck, despite the dangers it posed, was in many ways easier than methodically chewing through lumps of food. Elias imagined he might have a better night if he waited for her shift to end and caught her by surprise outside the diner.

The waitress shook her head and reached for his plate. "It's on us. Let me get this out of your way."

After she left, Elias counted out a four-dollar tip and tossed it onto the table. He went out to the parking lot and sat in his car, watching the diner through the front windows.

The waitress was the first to come out. When Elias saw her walking toward the front in her coat and hat, he got out of his car, slowly starting toward the diner.

She stopped by the doors and waved goodbye to a co-worker. Elias saw the two of them yapping to each other, and then the waitress went back into the restaurant and yapped some more.

Elias shivered in the cold air and muttered to himself.

She came to the doors again, half-turned around and said something to the other customer.

"Shut up," Elias hissed.

Finally she came outside. Elias crept along the shadows, maneuvering into the direction she was walking in, so that the two didn't meet until she was almost to her car. She spotted him suddenly, there in the darkness, and jumped back.

"Oh!" she exclaimed, and put a hand to her chest. "You scared me."

"Sorry," Elias said. "I think I left my gloves here. Did you happen to see them?"

"No, I didn't. But they might have fallen under the table." She gave him an apologetic smile. "I'm really sorry about the hair. I talked to the kitchen staff about it."

45

Elias looked into the woman's eyes, seeing the warmth there, the eagerness to appease. It was his move, now. He could talk in a calm, quiet voice, seduce her with sound and the intensity of his gaze—but the words didn't come, and the magnetism wasn't kicking into gear. Elias looked at the woman's neck, as if doing so could instigate his thirst and set things in motion. A lock of hair had come loose and hung against her throat. The harsh light of the streetlamp cast the lock in a gray tone, reminding Elias of the long gray hair trailing clumps of egg.

"It's no problem," Elias said, and his own words made the conversation seem unbearably tedious. He looked again at the woman's eyes. She was all wrong: her eyes, her voice, her hair. She was wrong because she wasn't Aarya, and Aarya was the one he wanted.

Aarya had been right about him, he realized. He had a "type," like one of those pathetic serial stalkers who sought women with a certain hair and eye color, simply because they reminded him of some girl who had jilted him in the past. Elias sought women his own age with long, dark hair, with energy and happiness in their eyes, because that was how he imagined Aarya would look now. He had wanted her, he had been angry at her for leaving him alone—and he had probably wanted to show her the depth of his pain.

He turned and left before the waitress could say more. She called after him, something about his gloves, but Elias only walked more briskly. He got into his car and drove away.

By the time morning came Elias was still upset, but not quite as angry. And when he drove into Pine Knoll and saw Aarya waiting for him across the bridge, dressed in an over-sized beige tracksuit and waving at him with her bandaged hand, his last bit of anger dissipated.

"It rained," she said as he approached. She took the ear buds out of her ear and shoved them into her pants pocket. "I tried to brush the water off of the rock, but it's still kind of damp."

"We don't have to sit on this rock every time we meet," Elias replied. "We can walk."

"No, let's sit first. It's warming up, and the frogs are singing, and—"

"I wouldn't call that 'singing,'" Elias replied.

"And I want to talk." Aarya hoisted herself onto the boulder and patted the spot beside her. "Sit here."

Elias complied.

"I woke up really early," Aarya said, "so I came out here and walked around the neighborhood. It's a lot different than it used to be. Remember the cornfield back there?" She made a wide gesture toward the trees. "It's all houses now. Whole neighborhoods full of two-story houses, and a bunch of parks and playgrounds."

Aarya lay on her back, looking up at the sky as she continued: "My house is still up there on the hill. It looks like a cop lives there. I've been past it twice, and both times there was a cruiser in the driveway." With a sudden smile, she looked at Elias and asked: "Remember the first time you came to my house? My dad had just come home from work, and he was passing you in the hallway, and he said 'Excuse me'—and you looked at him and said, 'Why, did you fart?'"

Elias chuckled. "Yes, I remember that day. We had that awful pizza, and you wanted to play Farkle the whole time. I was bored out of my mind."

"Were you? Well, Farkle was the game of math nerds."

"I hated math." Elias scooted farther down the rock and lay on his back beside Aarya. "Still do."

"Here." She rolled onto her side and handed him one

47

of her ear buds.

"I'm not sure why you think I want to put that thing in my ear, when you've just buried it in your own ear wax."

"It's fine. Check it yourself." Aarya shifted onto her back and added: "You never cared before."

"Well, I was a child and didn't know better. What am I listening to?"

"Theory of a Deadman. They did a great cover of 'Wicked Game.'"

"Wicked Game? Is it about Farkle?"

She scoffed as he fitted the bud into his ear. "No. It's about love. The narrator is mad in love with a woman, but he doesn't want to let himself fall. He's convinced that she's just going to break his heart. How else could it end?" Aarya watched him, waiting, as if for an answer, as the music played. .

"Anyway," Aarya said, looking again at the sky, "it's a little bit Gothic, and the theme is right up your alley. I thought you would like it."

Elias gazed at Aarya's face while he listened. Seeing her like this, close up and unguarded, gave him a strange sense of foreboding—dread mixed with an almost painful desire. Or perhaps it was just the mood of the song. Elias had always been easily moved by music. That was likely why he had stopped listening to it.

"Doesn't this feel like a blast from the past?" Aarya asked. "We used to lay around like this and listen to each other's music. I was always making CD mixes for you."

"Yes, I remember."

"I loved those times. Any time with you was usually good."

A sarcastic comment almost passed his lips, but Elias lost the urge to speak it. He lay there and looked at Aarya in silence.

"I'm going to make some music mixes for you," she

said. "Do you have a CD player?"

"A CD player," he repeated. "Sorry, dear, but CDs are outdated."

"Fine, but do you have one?"

"I do. Somewhere in my box of obsolete technology. I'll dig it out, just to please you."

"I'm going to be very intentional about the songs I choose. Keep that in mind when you listen." Aarya smiled at him with sly enthusiasm. It was a dangerous look, full of contentedness and hope. It stirred an anger that lurked somewhere deep inside Elias—yet he found that he could easily ignore it, and he continued to admire the flush of her face and the shine in her eyes.

"You know," he said, "even though you have an unflattering haircut, and you dress like a frumpy farm woman, and the outfit you're wearing right now couldn't look more like a potato sack even if it had the words 'Idaho Russet' stamped across the front . . . you're very pretty."

She wasn't offended, but only smiled a little more, and Elias basked in the warmth of her gaze.

After a couple more songs played against the backdrop of Aarya's eager explanations and backstories, they got up and walked back across the bridge. "Remember the little road that used to be over there?" Aarya asked, gesturing again toward the trees. "And there was that one house back there, all by itself? We went there when I was selling Girl Scout cookies. I was afraid to go by myself, so I asked you to come with me."

"Yeah, I remember. Is it still there?"

"No, it got torn down. That road is just another walking trail now. If you keep going on it, it winds around to the new neighborhoods."

Elias glanced up the road. "That's disappointing."

"Is it?"

"I liked that road." He could see, now, the dirt path leading into the woods, a wide path that had once been a road. "I wanted to live back here . . . with you."

Aarya looked at him, the trace of a smile spreading across her lips.

"I had all sorts of imaginings about it," he continued. "Remember how the road just came to a dead end? I wanted to have a house built at the end of that road, and live there with you. And it would be an exciting house with secret passageways and hidden rooms, and plants everywhere. And a hot tub, of course, since you liked them so much. And an ice cream maker."

"Wow. See, you do remember things."

Elias felt a sudden rise of discomfort, but suppressed it. He made a careful note of Aarya's expression as he spoke: "Even though we were really young, didn't you hope that someday we would end up together?"

Aarya's face sobered; the smile faded. "Yeah, I wanted us to stay together," she said quietly. "Until I moved away, and then . . . I thought about you, but I figured you would forget me."

"Why would I forget my only friend? Everyone else at school avoided me like the plague, because . . . ." Elias hesitated as a sudden tightness seized his chest. He waited for it to pass. "People knew that my stepfather was a creep," he continued. "They talked about it, and speculated, but no one did anything. It was always a stigma that I couldn't shake."

"You did forget me, though," she said. "Eventually."

"It wasn't forgetting. It was avoidance. I didn't want to think about it."

Aarya's eyes betrayed her sadness, even though her voice didn't. "I know."

They walked on, turning onto the dirt path and into the woods. Suddenly, Aarya said: "You can't stay a vampire."

"Why not?" Elias asked. "It's an easy life. It's safe. No one is stronger than I am."

"I'm stronger than you are," she countered. "And you can't avoid pain and victimization like this. The only difference is that you're the one causing it."

Elias felt himself wincing. He thought back to Aarya's threat: that she would take back every drop of blood he'd stolen. It had rattled him, at first, perhaps because she'd taken him by surprise and overpowered him, leaving him with an impression of her unpredictability and strength— yet he had preyed on someone only hours ago, with no consequence.

"You said that if I ever tried to bite anyone again, you would stop me," he said.

"Have I stopped you?"

The words struck Elias with an uncomfortable irony. He remembered his repulsion—or, at least, a complete lack of interest—with the woman from the diner, the turning of his thoughts toward Aarya and all she had ever meant to him.

"You haven't bitten anyone lately," she said, peering at him. "I would know."

"How?"

"Never mind how." She continued to study him, her eyes slightly narrowed, as if to focus more acutely. "If you feel like doing it, come see me."

"What will you do?" he asked.

"It depends."

The dirt path curved to the left, leading out of the woods and into a sprawling suburban neighborhood. A paved road led past houses still in prime condition and pristine sidewalks swept almost clean of autumn leaves. "Wow," Elias said. "This looks different." He gazed down the road at the green lawns and sparsely planted decorative trees. "This is really sad, actually. The big

51

forest back there is gone, too. Remember how we used to walk back there and see all those deer, and opossums, and foxes?"

"Probably dead now," Aarya replied. "You loved those animals. And bugs, too. You knew the name of every insect in the forest. I was always trying to swat them, and you were like, 'Oh, no, Aarya, that's just a Midwestern stink beetle,' or whatever they were called. I remember I got bitten by a spider one time, and I was looking all over the ground for it so I could stomp it to death, and you were pulling me away and saying 'Don't kill it. It just bit you because it was scared.'"

Elias didn't remember such an incident, but he supposed it was true. He had always been interested in insects and spiders, and had checked out every book on entomology from the local library.

"Remember the fort we had back in those woods?" Aarya continued. "Well, not really a fort, but a place where we used to hang out. And that one time, we brought my parents' portable grilling set and a jug of water, and we stole a couple of corn cobs from the field and boiled them."

"And it was field corn," Elias finished. "And we kept trying to eat it anyway, even though it tasted awful."

Aarya laughed, and Elias matched her with a smile. They continued to wander the neighborhood in the early morning quiet, passing the occasional early-morning jogger and dog walker, talking about times past and the inevitability of change.

The sun rose long before Elias returned home, and even though it illuminated the world in fine detail, Elias no longer found it uncomfortable.

The vampire expected his housemates to be asleep, but as he entered the lobby, he became aware of a figure standing at the far end of the the right-hand hallway. Elias looked up and felt a chill run through him. For a moment, he stopped breathing.

Dayna, the wendigo, stood there like a statue, watching him in silence.

Elias forced himself to draw in a breath. He called out a casual greeting: "Hi, Dayna."

She didn't respond, but only looked at him with an unsettling grin. Elias turned away and headed for his rooms. He stepped quietly, trying to listen for other sounds of movement—just in case Dayna should try to sneak up behind him.

Any encounter with the wendigo was unnerving. Dayna was not a night creature or a day creature, but was active at random hours. Her one consistency was that she preferred solitude; thus, Elias rarely ever had to see her. When he did, he was always struck with an inexplicable sense of fear.

Dayna had never done anything in particular to frighten him. His fear was, perhaps, a result of details related to her physique: her eyes, her smell, the general aura she gave off. Dayna had eyes that looked human enough, but they reminded Elias of the eyes of a snake: cold, blank, incapable of expressing feeling. Her scent was persistently foul. Sometimes she gave off a whiff of exceedingly bad breath, but more often she exuded a smell like that of a rotting corpse. The wendigo tried to veil those smells with fragrant soaps and perfumes, with little success.

Her eyes were not the only unsettling feature of her face. At a distance she looked fairly unremarkable, but on closer observance, one could see that there was something odd about her mouth. Her lips were so thin as to be barely visible, and her mouth itself was unusually wide. When she spoke, which she rarely did, she ducked her head so that her face was hidden behind her long hair. Elias had heard her voice, a soft, coarse sound that never really seemed like it was coming from her, but over time he realized that he had never seen the inside of that expansive mouth.

As he passed the kitchen, Elias heard Bruno's voice. He stopped and poked his head into the room. Bruno was alone, rummaging through the fridge and muttering to himself.

"Where's your son?" Elias asked.

"Sleeping, like I should be," Bruno replied. "Did you eat the bacon that was in here?"

"No."

"I need bacon."

Elias glanced back down the hallway. The wendigo had vanished, but Elias spoke in a quiet voice anyway, afraid of being overheard. "Dayna's back."

Bruno slammed the refrigerator shut. "So that's where it went. That skinny little ghoul could eat the whole kitchen and not gain a pound."

"I meant," Elias said, "that you should keep an eye on the boy."

Bruno scoffed. "Dayna won't mess with anything that's mine. Well, she probably ate the bacon, but she won't go so far as to touch my kid. Bacon can be replaced. Nobody cares about the pig that went into it."

Elias was already walking away. He was eager to sleep, and for the day to pass into night, and for the night to pass quickly into another morning with Aarya. It didn't matter, now, what her motivation was. He only cared that he enjoyed her company.

The next night was a productive one. Elias found himself less distracted and more determined to get ahead with his editing projects. He worked steadily through the hours, taking a short lunch break at midnight and hurrying back to his work. By the time Leitha came to his room at four o'clock, asking for help with a coding task, Elias had finished two nights' worth of projects.

"I just need you to check this assignment," Leitha said as he followed her into the office. "They sent it to test my skills, and I want to make sure it's my best. They're offering good pay."

Elias had stopped in the doorway. He pointed to the corner, where Luka sat playing with one of Leitha's scarves. "What is he doing here?"

"Bruno needed sleep. He hasn't slept well the past couple days." Leitha picked up the child and held him on her hip, looking smilingly into his eyes. "That's not your fault, is it, though? You're so quiet, I can't imagine you waking a beast who snores the way Bruno does."

Elias sat at the computer, his eyes still on Luka. "He's old enough to be able to talk, isn't he? I've only ever heard him say one word."

"Luka can talk; he just needs practice. He can say my name, but he says it in his own cute way: 'Lee-ta.'" Leitha looked again at the boy and coaxed him: "What's my name, darling?"

The boy looked at her, then hugged her and rested his head on her shoulder.

"He talks," she assured Elias. "I'll teach him to say your name next."

Leitha set the child on the floor, cooing at him and playing silly games such as "peek-a-boo" while she waited for Elias to check her work. He found himself glancing repeatedly at the two, initially with surprise at the seeming change in Leitha—but the more he thought about it, the more fitting it seemed that she could engage with a child. Leitha was, after all, only a wannabe monster. She behaved like a succubus, preying on men and draining them of their energy, but other aspects of her had remained all too human. Leitha had warmth; she

55

looked at Luka with genuine affection in her eyes, smiling as she tried to coax some delight out of him, and in response the child began to murmur and giggle, and even to speak: "More, Lee-tah! Again!"

Elias appreciated that she was too busy playing with Luka to flirt. "You're good with kids," he said.

"I'm good with men, too," she replied.

He suppressed a sigh.

"Just saying. I'm all right at coding, but there are things I'm expert at." Leitha paused, and added, "Vlad."

Elias threw an annoyed look in her direction. "Quit calling me that."

"Just trying to get under your skin," she said. "It's as close as you'll let me get."

When the task was finished, Elias drove early to Pine Knoll. The rusty red car wasn't in its usual place. Neither was Aarya; the rock was bare.

Within minutes, though, the Chevy rolled up behind him. Elias saw Aarya in the rearview mirror, smiling and waving.

"Take this," she said by way of greeting. She held out her hand to him, extending a small plastic box. Inside, Elias could see a cheap MP3 player and a pair of earphones.

Elias didn't move. He stared at her hand. The bandage was gone, and now he could see the damage he'd done to Aarya's flesh. His canine teeth had torn wide gashes in her skin, and though the wounds were healing, they were crusted over with a strange residue. "What's with your hand?" he asked. "Did it get infected?"

"No."

"Then why does it have all that gunk on it?"

"It's super glue. It was either that or stitches." Aarya held up her hand at his eye level. "You really did damage to this hand. It still hurts to move my thumb and finger."

He lowered his eyes; his face flushed. "Sorry about that."

Aarya extended the box to him again. "Take it. I thought this would be easier for you than going through all of your, whatever you called it—obsolete technology. I put a few different playlists on it."

Elias took the device out and examined it. "How do I know what I'm listening to? There's no display."

"Just turn it on and press play. If you want to see the playlists, you can hook it up to your computer. The USB is in the box. And if you want a specific playlist, you have to hold this button down. Here—I'll show you how to do it." She took the player from his hand. "I made four playlists: 'Relax,' 'Moody,' 'Upbeat,' and 'Kinda happy.'"

"Kinda happy? Why not just happy?"

She gave him a sly look. "Are you ready for that kind of happiness?"

Elias suppressed the urge to roll his eyes. "Are you ready to stop analyzing me?"

Aarya didn't look at him, but smiled faintly as she fiddled with the player. "Not yet."

6

As the day wore on, it brought other changes. Elias, having stayed awake long past sunrise, slept later than usual—and when he slept, he had nightmares.

Twisted, dark scenes played out in his mind. He dreamed of his childhood bedroom, the muffled sound of a man's voice, a fleshy face that he couldn't quite see. Though the details were blurry, the dream left him with a vivid sense of ugliness and despair. Elias woke with a grimace, his mind still filled with murmurs of the man's voice and the sour stench of his flesh.

Elias sat up. He swung his legs over the side of the bed. For several minutes he stared at the door to his room. The idea of going through that door seemed repellent; life and uncertainty were on the other side, waiting to devour him.

He sat with his head in his hands, trying to will the ugliness away.

Bruno had already been up for some time. In the kitchen, Elias found a half pot of coffee that had gone cold. He microwaved a cup and stood with his back against the counter, taking a careful sip and brooding over his dreams.

Vampires didn't have nightmares. They *were* the nightmare. They had only thirst, and their feelings switched primarily between hunger and the lack of it. The part of their minds in which nightmares bred was inert; it produced no imagery or emotion. This time Elias had spent with Aarya, the things she had compelled him to remember—they were activating the parts of him that were human, the parts that were vulnerable and afraid.

Bruno came in, ignoring Elias and heading directly for the fridge. He pulled out a loaf of bread and tossed two slices onto the counter.

Elias glanced at the dishes stacked beside the sink and the oil-smeared pan on the stove. "Didn't you already eat?"

"I'm hungry again," the werewolf replied. "It's getting to be that time."

"You didn't wash your dishes."

"No, because I'm going to use them again at lunch." Bruno smeared a thick slab of mayo onto one slice of bread, then the other. "Why are you up so late?"

Elias shrugged and sipped his coffee.

"You've been coming home after sunrise," Bruno said. "What's that about? You haven't been hunting, I know that. You're starting to stink like a human." He moved close to Elias and took a couple of sniffs. "Time to get out there for some fresh meat."

Elias moved away from him. "Meat is your thing, not mine."

The werewolf shoved the bread, turkey, and mayo back into the fridge, and tossed the butter knife into the sink. "Blood, then. Get yourself some mortal quaff."

"I don't know what that means," Elias replied in a tired voice.

Bruno picked up his sandwich and headed for the hall, but paused to look back at Elias with disdain. "It means get back on your game and be the hunter, instead of stinking like prey. When the full moon hits, you don't want me catching a whiff of you. I go by smell, not by sight. We might have an accident."

"It hasn't been that long," Elias replied. "I've gone for much longer, with no complaint from you."

"Well, something's off," Bruno said. "Maybe it's the stink of sunlight. You best keep to the night hours like the rest of us."

He walked away, leaving Elias to his pondering.

The vampire plugged away at his work for an hour, and then drove to the 24-hour market for groceries. He picked out items that would make small and simple meals: berries, pita and hummus, cheese and crackers, deviled eggs. Elias avoided going to the areas where employees were stocking shelves, and managed to avoid human contact by using the self-checkout lanes.

His work that night felt particularly boring. Elias found himself thinking often of Aarya—not in the longing, curious sort of way, but rather with irritation at the way she had shaken up his life. Being a vampire no longer seemed easy or mundane, and the idea of a life with monsters presented new anxieties. Bruno, who became increasingly wild as the full moon approached, was already making threats and thinking about his prey. The next full moon was still a week away. Between now and then, who knew what else would get under Bruno's skin—or into his "sniffer," as Bruno liked to say.

Images of Bruno's wild eyes and erratic moods haunted Elias throughout the night. There were always one or two nights a month when the werewolf came home with spatters of blood on his clothes. It had meant little to Elias; after all, the vampire also dealt in blood. He avoided Bruno at those times, telling himself that the werewolf was overwrought and excitable, and would get on his nerves. Elias had never paused to think about the person on the receiving end of Bruno's violence. Even though the werewolf had stated outright that he had killed, Elias had never taken the claims seriously; he told himself that Bruno was prone to exaggerate. Now, though, the reality of Bruno's cold-blooded crimes was starting to sink in, as though Elias was waking from a years-long trance. Bruno had killed. He may have even murdered Luka's mother. Viktor, too, had been aghast at the idea of making more vampires, and had surely left his victims to die.

Such thoughts made it difficult for Elias to stay on task. All he could think about were the killers living across the halls from him: Bruno, and most certainly Dayna. By the time he left the building with Aarya's MP3 player in hand, the vampire was consumed by a chilling anxiety.

Elias walked toward town, fitting the buds into his ear and switching the player to "Moody." He didn't feel, at the moment, that he deserved relaxation or even a dash of happiness. The vampire pulled a knit cap from his pocket and yanked it over his head. The early October night was particularly cold, but Elias walked on anyway, aimless and unsettled.

The music did little to soothe him at first. Aarya had added songs with titles like "The Curse," "In Need," and "A Soulmate Who Wasn't Meant to Be," songs that only enhanced the vampire's sense of quiet turmoil. Elias walked briskly, as if to escape something, but only ended up making a broad circle back toward the Woodlands complex.

In the dark of night, long before sunrise, he drove out to the Pine Knoll neighborhood. There he continued to walk. He covered the forest trails he'd walked with Aarya as a child, thinking of the joyful times they'd had together, the adventures and the long conversations that had given him his only real sense of friendship. He wandered through the tacky-looking suburban neighborhoods and reminisced about the woods and animals now lost to human development, the vast fields of corn that had given the golden-hour landscape a meditative glow.

As morning approached, Elias headed back to the foot bridge. For some reason, he didn't want Aarya to know that he had wandered this area by himself. He supposed he didn't want her to analyze his reasons.

The music in Aarya's playlist had finally quieted his mood. As the night had endured, the vampire found himself identifying with the melancholy tunes; he began to feel that there were people out there who understood him, who were singing to his loneliness and confusion. Elias got into the car and closed his eyes, listening for another minute before switching the player off. The problems that faced him hadn't changed since nightfall, but something about the music seemed to shift his perspective. Perhaps it was just the sounds of human voices, the narratives of human feelings. Something about the music had opened up a new emotion within him: grief for the people he had hurt. Like all of the people who had ever let Elias down, he had hurt those people instead of helping them.

That realization pushed Elias closer to the idea of change. Perhaps, as Aarya had said, he didn't have to be a vampire. Perhaps in that moment he was beginning to remember his true nature: that of a compassionate but deeply hurt human being. It was a terrifying, life-shattering notion, threatening to flow out of him in scents and actions that would draw the ire of monsters, yet there was a part of Elias that was tired of suppressing it.

Aarya's playlist had settled on a melancholy song about letting go, about letting one's true self flow outward. Elias switched off the brooding tune and started the car.

When he returned an hour later, he found Aarya waiting in the usual spot. She greeted him with her typical smile, and though Elias wasn't one to smile back, she noticed a certain moodiness about him as they walked the road toward her old house.

"What's the matter?" she asked. "You seem preoccupied."

Elias debated whether he should tell her anything at all. Aarya was a meddler; whatever he told her, she would use to meddle some more.

But he looked into her earnest eyes and felt his defenses easing. "My housemates are starting to notice that there's something different about me," he replied, deciding not to mention the nightmare.

"And?"

"And Bruno, the werewolf, kind of threatened me this morning."

"How? Are you in danger?"

"Probably not." Elias hesitated. "Maybe. It might have been an empty threat, but . . . somehow, I'm starting to seem human, and it bothers him."

"That's good, though," Aarya said. "It means you're actually changing. Instead of fearing it, you should take it a step farther."

Elias replied in a vexed tone: "It isn't fear, Aarya. I'm being practical. You don't know these people."

"It is fear, though, even if the threat is real." She peered up at Elias with a hint of concern. "Is Bruno the one who chased me when I came to your place? The big guy?"

"Yes, that's him."

"Who else lives there, besides the werewolf? Are there other vampires?"

"No. There used to be another one, but it's much more comfortable without him. Vampires generally detest each other. We are the most vain, jealous, and passive-aggressive beasts of the lot."

"Are there other werewolves?"

"No. There's Leitha. She's . . . sort of a succubus, but I'm not sure she qualifies. She preys on men, it's true, and she essentially drains the energy out of them, and takes advantage, and then she takes off with the contents of their wallets. But there's something human and vulnerable about her."

"Maybe she's on the edge," Aarya said.

"She probably is."

"Is it just the three of you, then?"

"No," he said. "There's Dayna, the wendigo."

"I don't know what that is."

"Neither do I," Elias admitted. "I've never seen what Dayna does. She disappears for long periods of time, and I don't know who or what she hunts, or what she craves, but . . . she gives off this sense like she's completely empty and craves everything. There's no speck of humanness in her at all."

"There must be," Aarya said, "somewhere."

"I challenge you to find it. Actually, I don't challenge you. It's best if you keep as far away from her as possible."

They walked on in silence for a while, up the steep road that led to the house. "Maybe it's not the same," Aarya said suddenly, "but I do know people who have done awful things, and recovered. The abbey has a prison outreach program—"

"So you said," Elias replied, somewhat irritably. The comment had reminded him of Zoua, and of the crime he'd committed against her.

Aarya guessed his thoughts. "That's right; I told you that Zoua was in that program."

"Yes, you mentioned it."

Another length of silence ensued, but Aarya didn't drop the subject. "Zoua had some issues with addiction . . . and . . . other things. She wanted to turn her life around

64

so she could go home and take care of her sons. She had two little boys. They're six and eight years old now."

Elias didn't reply. He looked straight ahead, quiet and expressionless.

"You should come to the abbey tonight," Aarya said. "We sometimes have medicine prayers in the evening. The nuns want you to come, so they can pray with you."

Elias gave her a look of disbelief. "With me?" he asked, and his voice sharpened. "What did you tell them about me?"

"I told them that you need the same kind of prayers that we make for people in the prison outreach program." Aarya looked coolly at him, not acknowledging the anger in his voice. "Even if you won't come to the ceremony, we should meet at the abbey next time. I can show you around, and we can walk around the downtown area. Most of the places we used to hang out at are gone. Our fort is gone, most of the forest is gone. They even leveled the hill where we used to go sledding."

"This area is fine," Elias replied tersely. "I have no interest in the abbey."

"Why? Does it remind you of something?"

"I'm already in a mood, Aarya. There's no need to provoke me."

"Am I provoking you? I'm not saying anything that you don't already know."

Elias looked at her. He found himself suddenly irritated by her nonchalance. "You're too careless," he said, "and you think too much of yourself."

"Maybe it's not about me, Elias," she replied. "Maybe I've always thought highly of you."

He stopped, looking at her with derision. "Why? Because I spared the life of a spider ten years ago?" Elias waited for Aarya to see the naivety of her assumptions, but her expression remained unchanged. "I'm not going to pretend that I haven't been naive, too," he said. "I'm just starting to realize what kind of people I've surrounded myself with, and what they're capable of. If Bruno had gotten hold of you, instead of me, he would have torn you to shreds. Your prayers and playlists full of sentimental songs won't change that, and they're not going to change me, either. They've just made me more aware of what I am."

"And what are you?"

Elias glanced at the houses that lined the street, at the windows still dark and shaded. "A killer, like you said," he said quietly. "I even had a moment when I realized that, and I felt sorry for the people I hurt, but I don't feel any compassion now." As he spoke the words, Elias realized that he meant them. The grief he'd felt, the regret, had slipped away after the music stopped. "I feel . . . a little bit of scorn, and relief that I didn't let myself become one of them."

Aarya's voice maintained its cool tone, but Elias saw a fleeting emotion in her eyes—anger, perhaps. "So, what? All of a sudden you're going to stay a vampire?"

Elias felt a light sneer playing on his face. "Is everything 'all of a sudden' just because you showed up and played a few songs? It's been ten years, Aarya, ten years—"

"Six. It's only been six years since I left."

"Fine," Elias snapped, "it's six, six whole years of monumental changes and . . . and events that you don't have the slightest clue about, and you're still talking about me like I'm some idealistic little boy who wouldn't even harm a spider."

"Maybe you still are that little boy," she replied. "It seems like you never bothered to grow up."

He scoffed at her. "You really are naive. This isn't a game of children."

"Then how come when I look at you, I can't stop seeing a frightened child?"

Elias lunged at her, suddenly, without meaning to. He lunged with bared fangs and threatening eyes—but even before he realized he was doing it, he found himself stumbling backwards. A white-hot pain spread through his face, and the smell of blood filled his nostrils. Elias raised a hand to his nose. His blood dripped through his fingers and spattered onto the dirt path below.

Aarya had punched him. It had happened so fast, he hadn't seen it coming. Now she stepped forward, muscles tensed, eyes burning with anger. "Come at me again," she said, "and I'll hit you ten times harder."

Elias made a small gasping sound, a whispered pain.

"What, are you bleeding?" Aarya asked, mockery in her voice. "Didn't I say that if you attacked anyone again, I would take back all the blood you stole?" She tilted her head aside, getting a better look at his face. "Just because we talk and laugh and listen to music together, it doesn't mean I've forgotten what you did. You're lucky all I did was hit you."

She sprung toward him, but stopped short as Elias stumbled backwards again. He caught himself and fumbled in his pocket, searching uselessly for something to staunch the blood with.

"You already killed one of my friends, Elias," Aarya said, her voice trembling. "You took her hope away, and you took her away from people who loved her. She has two little boys who have to grow up without their mom. She'll never get to make amends." Aarya's eyes spilled over with tears; her breaths were punctuated with quiet sobs. "Don't you dare ruin yourself, too, Elias. You didn't just kill one friend of mine; you're trying to kill two." She bent forward, lowering her face to look Elias in the eye. "Understand? I have loved you for years, and I have waited for years to find you again. If you destroy yourself, if you destroy my friend Elias, I won't forgive you. I will kill you. I will cut off your head off and bury it a hundred miles from your body, and I will drive a stake through that frightened, pathetic heart of yours, if you don't let go of my friend."

She turned and stalked back down the street.

It took some time for the flow of blood to stop, and for Elias to recover from his shock. He looked down and saw damp spots on the front of his black coat. His right hand was streaked with red. Elias swore under his breath and hurried back the way he had come.

Aarya had almost reached her car by the time he caught up to her. She must have heard his footsteps slamming against the pavement as he sprinted down the road, but she didn't look back.

"Aarya!" he called.

She stopped in the street and turned to face him, her eyes still hard with anger.

The vampire stopped a few yards away. He thought it best not to get too close.

As he stood there looking at her, Elias was struck once again by the notion that staying a vampire wasn't an option, no matter how much he feared the alternative of becoming a human and a weakling. Once again he thought, with conviction, that no matter what kind of woman crossed his path, he would never feel the desire to feed again.

"I'll go to the prayer ceremony," he said.

Aarya turned away and strode the last few steps to her car. As she opened the door, she glanced back at him and said: "Seven o'clock."

Elias watched until the red Chevy turned onto the highway, and then he let out a soft hiss of displeasure. Seven o'clock was early. The sun wouldn't even have set by that time. Once again, Aarya was pressuring him to go out in daylight—and once again, she seemed to have scored a victory against the vampire in him.

7

The sun had just slipped past the horizon, and a half-moon was visible in the clear sky, when Elias pulled into the lot at Achiravati Abbey. The digital clock display in his car read seven-twenty—too late for the prayer ceremony, or whatever hallowed event Aarya had tried to drag him into.

She was sitting on the courtyard wall, wearing a hooded sweatshirt and that pastel green monstrosity. Elias couldn't read her expression as she stood up and faced him, but she didn't seem particularly disappointed by his tardiness.

"Sorry I'm late," he said, though he wasn't the least bit sorry.

"No big deal. We can still go in."

Elias' sense of security deflated. "We didn't miss it?"

"Not at all," Aarya replied.

They walked across the courtyard, Elias going at an intentionally slow pace. "Also, I'm sorry I snapped at you," he said. "I mean that. I deserved to be punched."

She looked at him with quiet scrutiny, but said nothing.

"So . . . are these real nuns or what?" Elias asked. "Those shoddy cabins make it hard for me to take this place seriously. Those, and this lopsided court with the dollar-store Buddha statue."

"This place is a big deal," Aarya said. "It's only the second monastery for Buddhist nuns in the U.S."

"Then why is it so ugly? If it's such a big deal, you'd

think they would have made it look a little more appealing."

"It's a poor community, Elias. Yes, it's always nice to make places look beautiful, but there isn't a lot of money here. This place was built with donations and volunteers. It will get prettier as time goes by, but the community is already beautiful. It's full of beautiful intentions. That's all that matters."

"Still," Elias said, "I can see how people would show up, and get a glimpse of your ninety-cent Buddha, and decide that maybe this place isn't legit."

Aarya rolled her eyes at him. "Yes, it's a cheap statue, but it has a rich meaning." She paused in front of the fiberglass figure. "There's other significance to it. See how he's sitting with his left hand facing up, and his right hand touching the ground? That's the *bhūmisparśa* pose. It represents Gautama Buddha's final challenge before achieving enlightenment; he had to face the demon Mara, and overcome his insecurities and fears. I don't think it's the best statue for this kind of courtyard. There's another, more meditative pose, with the hands in the lap and the eyes closed, that I think would be more appropriate for a welcoming space like this."

Elias gazed at the figure's relaxed and alert figure, the half-open eyes that seemed to look directly at him. "It's appropriate for me," he replied.

Aarya led him into the right-hand building, where Elias found himself just as unimpressed by the interior; it was bland and boring as any of the office-like Lutheran and Methodist churches he'd stepped inside of. A richly decorated curtain blocked a doorway on the opposite side of the lobby. Elias heard chanting coming from beyond, and when Aarya pulled the curtain aside to let him in, he stopped at the sight of six bald nuns seated along the sides of an oriental rug, heads bent as they chanted in a near monotone.

He looked at Aarya. She waved him onward, and he stepped inside uncertainly. This room was less plain than the lobby. The walls were covered with colorful banners depicting figures and motifs that Elias didn't take time to examine. At the front of the room was a long table covered with lit candles, bells, and a seated statue of the Buddha.

The silver-haired woman who Elias seen outside the monastery was seated against the left-hand wall. She smiled at him and waved.

Aarya sat beside the woman and gestured for Elias to join them. He sat, leaning his back against the wall and listening to the chanting. The nuns, he realized, were reading the chants from little booklets that sat on little stands in front of them. *Cheaters*, he thought with a smug grin. Elias noted that all of the nuns were older, none of them younger than fifty. They were mostly light-skinned, and age had made them puffy and washed out, with pasty gray undertones—definitely well into the "potato phase."

Elias amused himself with such thoughts while the nuns continued their near-monotonous chant. After about ten minutes he looked at Aarya, raising a hand to his mouth and making an exaggerated yawn.

She pursed her lips and elbowed him.

The women chanted on, occasionally punctuating the singing with a bell and drum. After a while the song changed: It became more musical, the notes lifting and falling and lifting again, and Elias found himself actually enjoying the tune. It reminded him of the Ojibwe songs he'd sometimes heard as a child, when he rode his bike to the yearly pow wow just outside of town.

The chant ended, and the nuns started another monotonous string of words accompanied by the persistent clanging of a bell. Elias looked around the room, hoping to see a clock. If the time got too late, he could always excuse himself.

The clanging stopped. The voices softened and became musical again. Elias closed his eyes and leaned his head back against the wall, trying to enjoy the song before it mutated into another ghastly monotone.

Seconds later, he was asleep. Elias didn't know how much time passed while he slumbered. He was roused by the feeling of a hand on his shoulder and voices murmuring nearby. The vampire opened his eyes to see Aarya kneeling beside him, and the nuns gathered close.

Aarya gently nudged his shoulder. In a quiet voice, she said: "Lean forward a little."

Elias did as she asked, and she slipped her hand behind his back.

One of the nuns, the puffiest and most potato-like of the lot, placed her palm near his chest. Though her hand was inches away from him, Elias nevertheless felt the pressure of her touch. He looked at Aarya in mind alarm.

"It's okay," she said.

The nun began to chant—a sweet and lilting tune. As the notes rose and fell, Elias felt a sudden sense of grief moving within him.

It's just the song, he told himself. Elias had always been easily moved by music.

But once the emotion began to move within him, it wouldn't settle again. Elias felt his eyes begin to ache and tear up. His hands began to shake, and then his legs, and suddenly he was terribly cold, shaking all over. He opened his mouth to ask for a blanket, but all that came out was a light, airy sob.

The other nuns joined in the chant as Elias bent his head and tried not to cry. Aarya, too, was chanting very close to his ear, her voice soft and light. Her hand remained in place on his back, and the potato nun still seemed to hold his chest, as though the women were supporting his heart between the two of them—and Elias' heart actually felt sore, like a tensed muscle that had finally been allowed to relax. Though he didn't understand the words being said, Elias imagined that they spoke directly to his life. His past rose up once again before him, the pain and degradation of so many moments, and the bleak helplessness of realizing that no one would care, no one on Earth would ever step in. People gossiped and surmised and looked away, but didn't help. Elias' stepfather had an eye for people who would have helped. He made a point of avoiding them.

The group chanting ceased, and the nun began another solo chant. The decrease in sound did nothing to ease the experience for Elias. As he listened to the woman's voice, he suddenly remembered another figure from his past: Ms. Nielson, his first-grade teacher. He could envision her in vague detail: her short afro, her round glasses, the nerdy teacher cardigans she always wore. Elias pictured her standing at the front of the classroom by the rainbow-colored vowels and names of the week, smiling at the students—and then the concerned look in her eyes as she paused by Elias' desk and saw what he was drawing. Ms. Nielson was someone who would have helped. She had tried to, in fact. She had talked to the principal and the school social worker, but Elias insisted nothing was wrong. He was too afraid of his stepfather. The teacher didn't ask about it again, but reminded Elias that "I'm here to help."

Why, Elias wondered, had he forgotten that? Why did he suddenly remember?

The chill vanished from his bones, replaced by a wave of heat. Elias began to sweat. The soreness in his heart intensified, and his eyes began to tear up. *I will not cry*, he told himself. *Not in front of these people. Not in front of*

Aarya. He felt another small surge of anger at her—for her presumptuousness, for dragging him into this situation.

But the despair washed up and out of him anyway: a mixture of sadness and fear, guilt and shame, tearing through him in an unstoppable wave. When it came out, it began as a soft weeping, as tears rolling down his cheeks. And then his nose began to run, and the weeping escalated into a messy cacophony of racking sobs, sweat, and snot.

As his mind continued to delve into those awful moments, Elias didn't believe that a few bars of chanting and the touch of a hand would make those moments less painful. Yet, somehow, they did. As the group finished its last round of prayer, Elias wiped his nose on the underside of his sleeve, trying to clean his face before lifting his head. With trepidation he looked at the solo nun (and that was how he would try to think of her: the solo nun, instead of the potato nun).

"Thank you," he said, with some embarrassment. He nodded a silent thanks to the others, and then he addressed Aarya without looking her in the eye, whispering: "Where's the bathroom?"

She led him to the men's room. Elias was relieved to find that it was a single toilet, and that he could lock the room. Though there were no other men at the abbey, he disliked the idea that someone could walk in on him.

As soon as he slid the bolt into place, Elias slid to his knees on the bathroom floor. He put his face in his hands and sobbed again.

At some point he became aware of his disheveled appearance. Elias went to the sink and balked at the sight of his red, puffy eyes and snot-crusted nose. He hurried to grab some paper towels, but found a useless hand dryer instead. The vampire splashed his face with water, scrubbed the mucus from his jacket sleeve, and crouched down to dry himself in the stream of hot air.

Once he was clean, and when the puffiness had receded from his eyes, Elias went out to say goodnight to the nuns. He thanked them again, mostly keeping his head down and his gaze on the floor—out of humility, he assured himself, rather than embarrassment. One of the nuns talked to him for a few minutes. She probably talked about prayer and cleansing and other spiritual things, but Elias nodded without being able to focus on the words.

Aarya followed him outside. "You don't have to walk with me," Elias told her, still unable to look her in the eye. "It's dark out."

"Come home with me," she said. "It would be better if you stayed at our place tonight."

Elias looked at her in surprise. "'Our' place?"

"I'm living at Beth's house. Beth is the woman who was sitting with us during the puja."

"The old lady," he said.

Aarya gave him a scathing look. "Yes, she's older. Really, Elias, it would be better if you came with us, instead of going back to . . . ."

Elias caught her meaning. "Right. You're going to sleep, though, and I'm not."

"I'll stay awake," she replied. "And if I fall asleep, and you get bored, you can just let yourself out."

He hesitated, wondering if perhaps the two of them were being too naive. "The idea of sleeping with a vampire doesn't scare you?"

She countered: "The idea of sleeping with werewolves and wendigos doesn't seem to scare *you*, even though it should. Especially tonight."

She had a point, Elias supposed. Even if going home with Aarya wasn't the best idea, being vulnerable in front of monsters was pure stupidity.

Beth came outside with a sympathetic smile, repeating Aarya's invitation to stay the night at her home. Elias accepted. The old lady drove while Elias and Aarya sat together in the back of her Buick.

The ride was mostly a silent one. At some point Aarya reached over and held Elias' hand, lightly wrapping her fingers around his.

Elias tensed. He looked down at her fingers curved around his, at the contrast of her brown skin against his deathly pale flesh, and stiffly pulled his hand away.

Aarya smiled.

Beth's house was a small two-story not far from downtown. The exterior was decorated with numerous planters, strung lights, and garden signs bearing messages of positivity and welcome. Elias dozed off during the last few minutes of the drive, and woke to the sight of a gleaming porch and a cheesy wooden sign entreating him to "Gather on our porch; sit long, talk much, laugh often."

He followed the women onto the first step, and as Beth opened the door in front of him, he froze.

Elias felt in his lungs that same sensation of mist, of some filmy substance that made it suddenly hard to breathe. Aarya paused in the doorway and turned to look at him. "Are you all right?" she asked.

"I don't know if I should go in," he said.

Aarya murmured something to Beth and came back outside, closing the door behind her. She stood on the front step beside Elias. "What are you worried about?"

"It's been a long time since I went into a person's house." He paused. "I'm worried . . . ."

"About what?"

In truth, Elias wasn't sure what had stopped him, but he chose the most logical explanation: "I can control myself around people," he said, "but . . . after whatever happened at the monastery . . . I feel like I don't know myself."

"You're afraid you'll bite me? Or Beth?"

"Maybe. I don't know."

She glanced back at the doorway. "It must be hard to go into someone's house, like you're just an ordinary person going for a visit. It's another step, isn't it?" Elias didn't answer, so she continued: "We've been hanging out together these past few days, and you've been okay."

"I don't feel like myself," Elias replied.

"But I don't think you're going to harm me. Are you? If you start to feel that way, you can leave." Aarya let him ponder the idea for a few moments, and then beckoned him. "Come inside."

Elias was unsurprised to find the interior of the house decorated in the much the same way as the outside, like it had been personally tended to by Martha Stewart and Pollyanna. The only aberration was Aarya's room on the upper floor. It was a barren space, with little more than a dresser and a bed. "Are you practicing to become a nun?" Elias asked. "This looks like the room of someone who's taken the poverty vow."

"No," Aarya replied. "I just don't have much, and I probably won't stay long. I don't want to get too settled."

"What's this?" Elias pointed to a metal crucifix that hung above the dresser. "Is this meant for me? Crosses don't really ward off vampires, you know. That's all myth."

"I know."

"This is a Christian symbol. I thought you were a Buddhist."

"I'm not anything," she said. "I admire Christ and the Buddha—and other spiritual figures too, but those are the two I'm most familiar with. I used to read the gospels and the Dhammapada whenever I was having a hard time, and they always helped me. I still read them."

"The Dhamma what?"

"The sayings of the Buddha."

Elias sat down on the bedspread. "I feel like this is a trap. You invite me to your room, and say we're going to stay up and chat, or whatever, but there's no furniture except for a bed."

"You were falling asleep. Do you want to rest some more?" Aarya sat on the bed beside him. "Cleansing ceremonies can be exhausting."

"No kidding." Elias paused, thinking back to his meltdown. "That nun . . . the one who had her hand on my chest—well, she didn't really have it on my chest, but it felt like she did. It felt like . . . ." He trailed off, not knowing how to explain.

"Did it feel like she was moving your energy around?" Aarya asked.

"I guess so. What's her deal? Is she even human?"

Aarya chuckled. "Yes, very. That's Vela. She's a Qigong master. Before she became a nun, she taught Qigong and did healing sessions. She still does them at the monastery, but one of her students took over her practice."

"What's Qigong?"

"Well . . . it's like a movement meditation. I don't know how to explain it. Vela did a session with me once, and I felt the same way—like she was moving things around inside of me." Aarya gave Elias a smiling but serious look. "You should talk to her some time. Seriously, even listening to her voice is incredibly calming."

"I wouldn't call her voice 'calming,'" Elias replied. "It was more like she beat me up and wore me out. Where are you going to be, if I'm in here sleeping?"

Aarya shrugged. "Wherever. I can sleep down in the living room. When you wake up, you can come and wake me too." She didn't look the least bit tired, Elias noted; she seemed energized, yet relaxed, and her face seemed to glow softly in the weak overhead light. "Or we can talk, if you want," she added.

The weight of another conversation seemed too much. He would have rather slept, and avoided it, but there were questions that Elias yearned to find answers to, fears he needed to address. He stared down at the panels of the laminate floor, unwilling once again to look at Aarya. "What will happen to me," he said, "if I stop biting people? Won't I die?"

"I don't know. That's up to you."

"Is it? I don't feel like it is."

"People can stop being vampires, Elias," she said gently. "A lot of people say it's not a reversible condition, but it's not true. I've seen people do it."

"Really. Like who?"

Aarya hesitated, as if she was ready with an answer, but wasn't sure whether to say it out loud. "You met one of them tonight."

"Who? Beth? Or one of the nuns?" Elias thought back over the group of pasty-faced women. "Was it the potato nun? I mean, the nun who had her hand on my chest?"

"No."

"It's you," he said. "You told me you were bitten."

"No, not me. I'll introduce you to her later." Aarya looked into his eyes searchingly, and Elias maintained the impression that she was still deciding how much to say to him. "It's not just her. A lot of the people in our prison outreach program decide to use the Buddha teachings to find their way out of . . . troubled lives."

"I'm not becoming a Buddhist."

"It's not about Buddhism," she said. "There's more than one path to becoming a mahatma."

"A what?" Elias asked.

"A great soul. I think that it's the destiny of each soul to become great, even if it takes multiple lifetimes."

"You talk like you think yours is already great."

Aarya flashed a wry grin. "One should first establish oneself in what is proper. One may then teach others, and lecture until the listener is annoyed and bored half to death, and not be blamed."

"Is that a Buddha quote?"

"Pretty much."

"And what are these other paths to become a mahatma?"

"Compassion," she said. "Honesty. Self-reflection. Not harming others . . . those are the bases of a lot of major religions."

"Are they?" Elias replied. "I thought that ego, power, and persecution were the bases."

"They can be. Everything can be abused."

Elias lay back on the bed, folding his hands behind his head. "Enlighten me, then, without abusing the precepts. How great have you become? Do you consider yourself a mahatma?"

"No."

"Why not?"

"Well, first of all, mahatma is a given title. You know, like Mahatma Gandhi."

"Oh, I see," Elias said, casting her a wily look. "Wasn't Gandhi racist?"

"He was, when he was young," Aarya admitted. "But, Elias, that's the point: People change. They learn from other people, they admit their mistakes, and they keep working toward becoming better. You don't just start out as a great person. You're allowed to be ignorant, and to make mistakes, but you're expected to learn and grow— for your own good, and everyone else's. And Gandhi did that, but he was never perfect, because he was human.

You're never going to be perfect."

"Neither are you. Sorry to disappoint you."

Aarya ignored the comment. "There's a quote from The Dhammapada that says, 'Think not lightly of goodness, that it will not come to you, for a water jar is filled by the falling of water drops. So the sage fills himself with goodness, soaking up little by little.' Change takes time." Aarya lay on the bed, facing Elias with her head propped up on her elbow. "There's a matching quote about what happens if you keep committing acts of evil, but I can't remember how it goes. It's the same principle, though. Little by little you poison yourself, until the poison grows into duhkha."

"What's that?"

"Suffering. Contempt, hopelessness, pain. The state you've been living in ever since you were bitten, and ever since you gave up being human." Aarya paused, as if to let the words sink in. "It's what tipped Zoua over the edge. When you bite people, you share your duhkha with them. And if you keep doing it, it's going to get worse, for them and for you."

Elias avoided her gaze, looking instead at the bedspread. "Is that why you're letting me in your house, and spending time with me, even after what I did to your friend?"

"Partly." Aarya waited until Elias looked at her again, and added, "You're allowed to be forgiven, Elias, if you quit and try to make things right."

"How? After killing someone . . . after damaging people's lives . . . ."

"It's not impossible. There's a quote—I'm not sure if it's from the Dhammapada, but—"

"Are you going to throw quotes at me all night?"

"I'll give it a rest after this. It goes something like, 'Even if someone has killed a thousand innocents, if that person is genuinely working to follow the path of righteousness, they become blameless.' A lot of people, especially the people we talk to in prison, think that there's a point so low you can't rise from it. But you can always rise, a little at a time. It's hard work. Can't you see yourself rising out of being a vampire?"

"I don't know if I would call that 'rising.'"

"And what about your roommates?" she asked. "With the right guidance, is it possible for them?"

"They don't seek guidance."

"People often don't," Aarya replied, "until they fall too far."

Elias sighed. "Leitha might have a chance. She's young, and she's more insecure than evil. She just needs to grow up a little."

"And what about your stepfather?" Aarya asked. "Is it possible for him?"

Elias looked at her in stony silence.

Once again, he found himself becoming irritated by her presumptions. He wanted to say: *It's so easy for you, isn't it, to forgive people who never laid a finger on you?* But he kept quiet, knowing that any challenge would result in another of her self-satisfied lectures.

Elias' gaze drifted to Aarya's neck. He became suddenly fixated on it, but couldn't decide what he wanted to do with it. The angry part of him wanted to sink its teeth in, to make her gasp in pain. That part of him was weak and nearly incapable, yet it maintained a stubborn presence.

"You keep looking at my neck," Aarya said. "Do you want to bite me?"

"Yes," he replied softly. "Sometimes."

She remained unfazed. "It must be hard for you to be close to humans," she said. "You must get the urge to drink."

"It's not like that," Elias said.

"What is it like, then?"

He hesitated, trying to find within himself the real reasons behind his impulses. "I don't think it's about drinking. It's not about filling myself. It's about draining other people. I want to bite you because I'm mad."

"Why?"

Elias didn't reply.

"This morning," she said, "when you came at me, were you going to bite me?"

"No. I wanted to scare some sense into you. You're too cool-headed for your own good."

"Hm. Well, it was a noble effort." Aarya paused, and added: "I thought tonight's prayer went well."

"It was hard," Elias said. "You're ruining my life."

"That's a good thing, though, isn't it?" she asked. "Now you can make a better life."

"There are things I like about the way I live," Elias said.

"Like what?"

He thought over the things about his lifestyle that satisfied him: *Security. My leather couch. My paycheck.* With those comforts, though, came a set of fears: the fear of being found out, of being turned on by his own pack of monsters, and other unnamed fears buried too deep to be identified. Mixed in with those anxieties was the ugliness of the things he'd done in the dark hours of night, and the gross feelings that stirred within him, unresolved and festering.

Elias couldn't put such thoughts into words. He rolled onto his back and sniffled, fighting back the onset of tears. His sudden grief annoyed him; he wasn't even sure what had saddened him.

"Get some rest, Elias," Aarya said softly. "I can see you're tired."

84

"I'm not in any state to sleep."

"Here." Aarya got up and went to the dresser. She came back with a tiny MP3 player, a slightly more expensive version of the cheap thing she'd given to Elias. "It will help you rest," she said, handing him the earphones. Elias placed one of the buds into his ear, and Aarya said: "Both of them."

He fitted the other piece into his ear. As Aarya fiddled with the player, she said, "I'm making more playlists for you because I missed a bunch of songs. I couldn't download them because they were connected to my old email address—but I have them now."

She climbed back into bed beside him and lay on her side, looking into his eyes.

The music began, a sad, lilting tune that did nothing to quell Elias' anguish. The notes followed a repetitive, vaguely shifting pattern that seemed to encourage a kind of release, until at last the words began, asking for the bliss of sleep, singing of the weariness of grief and the respite of love.

Despite his efforts to stay awake beside Aarya, Elias felt himself pulled into slumber. The song seemed to speak directly to him, soothing and entreating him, speaking of a childhood love hidden away and re-discovered on such a night as this—and he thought he saw the same message in Aarya's eyes, bright and penetrating in the dim light.

"You're doing this on purpose," Elias said softly.

Through the soft, soothing tones, Elias heard her ask: "Doing what?"

He didn't answer. He closed his eyes and slept.

8

The following night ended with monsters. Aarya wanted to do something "different," so she and Elias wandered one of the local parks until closing and debated what to do next.

"Let's go to the Anokatan haunted house," Aarya suggested as they walked back to Elias' car. "They're open three nights a week all month, and I think they don't close until midnight. It's actually scary. The high school puts it on, and the kids do a really good job—and you can buy popcorn and hot chocolate for only a dollar."

"High school haunted houses are cheesy," Elias replied. "But if you like it . . . ."

"I bet you won't think it's cheesy once you're inside," she challenged him. "I bet you'll scream at least once."

Elias didn't take her seriously. His self-satisfaction only increased as they stood in line on the county fairgrounds, outside the building where teachers and students had built a labyrinthine system of spooky scenes and macabre costumes. As he stood on the outskirts, munching on a packet of one-dollar popcorn and trying to ignore the excited jabbering of children, a teen in a "Scream" costume came at him with a plastic knife and pretended to stab at him.

"Oh, how horrifying," Elias said in a bored voice. "Someone's trying to kill me with cosplay."

Another specter appeared a few minutes later, a zombie-like creature with a rotting face. Elias posed with the costumed teen while Aarya snapped a photo with her phone.

"Lovely," she said, showing him the display on her screen: Elias posing with wide eyes and a frightening smile, his long canines exposed, mimicking the lidless eyes and lipless mouth of the creature beside him.

Once inside, the two found themselves confounded by the darkness of the place. Elias reached out, his fingertips trailing along plywood walls as he tried to find his way. "The scariest thing about this place," he said, "is that in order to get through it, I have to keep putting my hands in the same spot where a hundred kids have been sticking their snotty little fingers."

A few feet ahead of him, the end of the hall was illuminated by a sudden burst of light: A teenage boy sat in a makeshift electric chair, screaming and writhing over the loud zapping of the chair, fake blood trailing from the wire-laden cap on his head.

Elias shouted and jumped back.

The hall went dark again, quiet except for the sounds of Elias's panting and Arya's laughing.

"Okay," Elias said breathlessly, trying to feel his way around the corner, "that scared me."

"I told you so," Aarya said behind him. "That was only the first room, Elias, and you already screamed. There's like, twelve more."

They made a slow trek through the maze, making brief and heart-pounding acquaintances with vampires, zombies, and wild-eyed lunatics. Aarya held onto his arm as they stumbled through the dark. As the jump scares became repetitive, Elias found himself focusing less on the contrived terrors of the show, reveling instead in Aarya's closeness and the quickening of her breath in his ear.

His editing work went smoothly that night. Although he kept thinking back to his adventure with Aarya, Elias was hardly distracted from his work. Rather, he felt focused and refreshed. He finished ahead of schedule and spent time in the lab, reading and making notes; then he worked on transferring Aarya's playlists to his cell phone.

He met her the next night at the abbey. The plan had been to walk from the abbey toward town, but Elias pulled up beside her in the lot and beckoned through the open window. "Get in," he said.

She slipped into the passenger seat and pulled on her seat belt. "Where are we going?"

"Cinnabar Park. Is that all right?"

"I don't know what that is."

"Good," he replied.

They drove across town to the sound of Aarya's 'Upbeat' playlist, to a small park that boasted walking trails and spectacular falls. The waterfall itself was pitiful, little more than a stream making a simple one-story drop. Elias and Aarya took the path away from the falls, toward the foot bridge that led over the water.

A chain-link fence bordered both sides of the bridge, rising just a few inches above Elias' head. The gating was decorated with a multitude of padlocks bearing expressions of love and commitment, placed there by locals who wanted to make a public display of their feelings. Many of the locks were in the shape of a heart, and there were some unique displays here and there, including a skull-themed lock that bore the words "'Til death" in white ink, and one stamped with a "New York Insane Asylum" logo on which someone had scrawled "You drive me crazy (in a good way)."

"I didn't know we had one of these around here," Aarya said, pausing to examine the asylum-branded lock. "I've only seen something like this on a Korean TV show."

"Americans love cheesy displays of affection just as

much as anyone else." Elias gestured ahead. "There's a spot right over there where we can sit for a while, if you want."

As they came to the end of the bridge, he pointed to a large, flat rock in the middle of a grassy field. "Look," he said. "Our Pine Knoll boulder has a twin. Can we sit for a while?"

"Sure."

Elias stretched out on the cool stone, lying on his back and looking up and the first hints of starlight. "We're going to have clear skies the next few nights," he said. "Do you know when the Draconid meteor shower is supposed to happen?"

"Never heard of it," Aarya replied, lying beside him. She turned on her side, gazing at his face. "Are you tired? You've been getting up early."

"No, I'm not tired. And I haven't been getting up early. I only sleep eight hours a day, at the most. Nine to five, ten to five . . . I just wanted to sit for a while because I want to talk."

"About what?"

Elias was silent for a while. "You asked me if I thought my stepfather could . . . stop being the way he is," he said. "It bothered me. I keep thinking about it, and here's my answer: He would put on a show of decency, and act all polite and good, but he would be secretly picking out someone who's easy to prey on. That's how he is. I've never seen any other part of him. He moved us here when I was five, supposedly for a job, but I think it was to isolate me. My mom's sisters and parents all lived near us in Stockholm. I'm sure that's why."

"Well," Arya replied, "I won't deny that he's shit."

"He's a sociopath," Elias replied. "But he doesn't get branded as a monster. How come serial killers and psychopaths get to be branded as humans, and people like me are monsters?"

"There's nothing supernatural about being a sociopath," Aarya said. "Your body doesn't change. You don't grow fangs or claws, or a whole new digestive system because of it."

"Still. It seems like an unfair stigma." He looked over at Aarya and asked: "What about you? Could you forgive your uncle?"

"I could," Aarya replied readily, "if he actually changed. If he realized what he did, and how foul it was, and the amount of damage he caused, and if he actually made an effort to change himself into a better person."

Elias pondered her words. "That doesn't seem right to me. You shouldn't get to damage other people for years, and suddenly say 'Oh, I guess that was wrong, sorry about that,' and act like everything's fine."

"It's not like that. People should pay for what they did." Aarya looked him over. "The person who bit you, and who turned you—did that person remind you of your stepdad?"

Elias answered without hesitation: "No. He had a different energy. A lot of anger. I don't know who it was; it happened in the dark, and I never really saw him. But I remember knowing that something terrible was happening to me, and trying not to give in to it—and then it just seemed easier to embrace it. It seemed powerful, actually. Like embracing it was a revenge on everyone who hurt me." He looked at Aarya's neck, saw nothing of note— not a scar, or a mark of any kind. "When were you bitten?"

"I've been bitten more than once. I seem to attract vampires."

Elias didn't ask what she meant. As someone who had tried to prey on her, he supposed he already knew.

They were quiet for a while, and then Elias said,

"That's all I wanted to talk about. I just wanted to answer your question."

"Okay."

"We don't have to stay on this rock. We can walk down to the polluted swimming hole, or go look at the construction site that's at the end of the path, or whatever."

"We should go out on the town tonight," Aarya said.

"Where?"

"Mmmm . . . ."

"Hair salon," Elias suggested. "For starters. I'm sorry to say it, but whoever cut your hair did a horrendous job. They gave you a Caesar crop. And even though there's hardly any bangs, they managed to make them crooked. And—"

"They're not crooked," Aarya cut in. "They look that way because I have an uneven hairline."

"If they look crooked, then they're crooked." Elias reached out to straighten her hair, but thought better of it and pulled his hand back.

"You should fix your hair, too," she said. "Or at least put your head up, so your hair isn't always hanging over your face. Half the time when I try to look at you, all I see is a white curtain."

"I like being hidden," Elias replied.

"It looked better when it was short. I could see your face then."

"Your hair needs more attention, believe me," he said. "And you should get rid of this jacket." He reached over and tugged at her sleeve. "You would look good in a deep green, a forest green or something, but this hideous pastel color reflects off your face and makes you look pale and sickly, and . . . like you're about to vomit."

"Thank you, Elias," she said.

"Even if you're not trying to look like a runway

model, you don't have to wear the world's ugliest clothes on purpose," Elias added. "Even the nuns wear vibrant colors that make them look good. You're the only one who looks like a frump. That big, baggy, beige sweatsuit has to go, too."

Aarya looked at him with a small gasp. "That's my most comfortable outfit!"

"No, Aarya, you have to get rid of those. The ugly jacket and the ugly sweatsuit. If you do that, I will get my hair cut however you want." He turned his head to gaze at her. "I will stop being a vampire if you get rid of your ugly clothes." Elias waited until she looked back at him, and added: "Let's go shopping. I will buy you a comfortable sweatsuit, and I will buy you another jacket." He hesitated, unsure whether to ask the question that had begun to nag at him. "When did you get this jacket?"

"I bought it at the thrift shop."

"When?"

Aarya, too, was hesitant to speak. "After Zoua died," she said at last.

"Because she was wearing yours."

"Yeah."

Elias saw the trace of anguish in Aarya's eyes. This time, it didn't irritate him. "I'm sorry, Aarya."

She was quiet for a while, just lying there and looking back at him. "Okay," she said.

"What should I do?" Elias asked.

"What do you mean?"

"I mean, what should I do about what I did to people? Isn't there some Buddha quote about making amends for the shitty things you've done?"

"I honestly don't know what you should do," Aarya replied. "Aside from just trying to be a decent human. Because . . . in cases of assault, the perp should confess, and serve the punishment. But what would you say if you turned yourself in? That you're a vampire? You would end up in psychiatric care, and the women and their families would still never know what happened. People aren't aware of this world; they don't know that vampires exist."

Elias tried to imagine such a confession. He envisioned himself at a police station, trying to turn himself in. *I bit people and turned them into vampires. My bite amplified their misery so much that some of them died.* Aarya was right; he would be committed for sure. The realization eased some of the anxiety he'd begun to feel about facing the people he'd harmed, the family and friends he'd hurt by extension. He couldn't help feeling grateful that Aarya had come up with an excuse not to face them.

But then she said, "The best you could do is tell the police that you're the person who bit those two women in the crime reports—the one at the park, and the one at the arcade."

Elias' sense of relief deflated. "I'm afraid to. I'll get branded as a creep."

"Well, that's fair, you *were* being a creep."

He tried to think of a good reason not to make such a confession. He had plenty of selfish reasons: Punishment, embarrassment, the possibility that someone would take revenge on him. "I suppose," he said, "that you believe all that stuff about karma—that we carry karma from one life to the next, and that we have to take actions to fix it."

"I'm really not sure about different lifetimes," Aarya replied, "but the idea makes sense. I do think people internalize the evil they've done. I think it harms them, and keeps them from achieving greater heights, even if they think they've benefited from it."

"That sounds very Buddhist."

"Well, a lot of Buddhist ideas make sense to me.

That's why I spend time at the abbey."

"Don't become a nun, though," Elias said. "Please. Practice Buddhism, or Christianity, or any other religion, if you want. But don't become a nun."

"Why?"

Elias felt a sudden anxiety, a constricting of this throat. He took a breath, waiting for it to pass. "You know why," he said softly. "Someday, when I deserve you, I want to be with you."

She looked back at him wordlessly while he tried to read the emotion in her eyes. He saw feeling there, but it was indecipherable, too multi-faceted for interpretation, and so Elias lay there and gazed into her eyes until he nearly felt lost in the essence of her—and then she shattered it by speaking.

"Elias."

"What?"

"Christie's Hair Salon is still open. Let's go now."

Elias took a few moments to process what she was saying. He released a quiet sigh. "You're changing the subject."

She smiled.

"No, you're right," Elias said. "It's too early. And that hair needs attention." He sat up. "Let's get to it."

The salon wasn't far from the park. The drive only lasted a couple of songs, and then Elias was walking into the salon after Aarya, ducking his head and hiding his face. It was a habitual reflex, and his discomfort was exacerbated by the salon's bright lights.

A rack full of sample portraits stood near the front desk. Aarya looked them over, and then handed one of the style guides to Elias. "Here. Hairstyles for blonds."

He picked a booklet from the opposite side and shoved it toward her. "Here: Styles for Indian women who cut their hair too short."

They sat beside each other in the lobby chairs, glancing at each other's booklets and making suggestions. "Don't get anything nerdy," Elias warned.

Aarya ended up choosing "messy undercut pixie," which the hairdresser cut and styled with a light gel. Elias was still looking through his booklet when the barber cape was slipped from Aarya's shoulders. "Much better," he said as she came back to the lobby area. "Sorry to disappoint you, Aarya, but you're pretty."

She gave him a cool smirk and sat beside him. "What did you decide on?"

"Nothing yet."

"Elias, it's been twenty minutes!"

"Fine, but yours was easy," he said. "All the decent styles are in the women's catalog, and the men look like douchebags. Look at some of these haircuts."

Aarya pointed to a portrait at the bottom of the page. "Medium layered waves," she read aloud. "That would be a good look for you, Elias." She tapped her finger on the photo. "Get this one. If you do, I'll get rid of my ugly sweatsuit."

"And the jacket."

"Deal."

He sat in the barber's chair and gave the picture to the stylist, who started by combing Elias' hair—always a strange, intimate feeling, Elias thought, but one that no longer bothered him—and then chopped away at it, letting the blond locks fall to the floor.

When Elias finished, Aarya greeted him with a delighted smile. "Elias!" she exclaimed. "I can actually see you."

The stylist, a middle-aged man with a haircut nearly identical to the one Elias had chosen, stopped sweeping and called out: "It suits him, doesn't it? It's a perfect cut for his face type."

95

Elias leaned toward Aarya and whispered: "Let's leave before he gets too friendly."

They paid and went back to the car. Aarya's smile was still plastered on her face. As she got into the passenger seat, she looked at Elias with a chuckle and said, "You look really different."

"Let's get your new clothes," he replied.

"We can't. The stores are closing."

"There's a fancy grocery store around here with a clothing section off to one side. They don't have much, but what they have isn't bad. They have a great dessert counter, too."

"Oh. That new, expensive place, right? I haven't been in there yet."

"Good. Another new adventure."

They went to the grocery, a sprawling, busy place whose front doors opened into an expansive bakery display. Aarya crept around the cases at a slight crouch, peering at the dozens of types of donuts, mousses, and cakes. "I just want to look, because everything's so pretty," she said. "I'm in the mood for seaweed rolls. You can get a dessert." She straightened up and poked a finger into Elias' side. "You need the calories. Look at how skinny you are. If there's a strong wind when we walk outside, you might blow away."

"I'm actually very muscular," Elias replied.

"You're not. I've felt your muscles, remember?"

He led Aarya to the clothing section, where she picked out a long black-and-white plaid jacket and a fleece pullover with matching pants. "It's cut a little too wide, but it looks good on you," Elias said, as Aarya tried the jacket on in front of the dressing mirror.

She slipped the coat back off. "I didn't know you were such a fashionista."

Elias was holding the green jacket. He lifted it and

96

said, "We can throw this in the trash on the way out."

"No, Elias!" Aarya protested. "You don't just throw clothes in the trash. It's still in good condition. I'll donate it."

"Fine, fine. Someone else can look like they're about to vomit. Let's get food."

The last traces of sunset had vanished by the time they headed back to the park. Aarya sat on the boulder across from Elias, carefully picking up a slice of ginger with a pair of wooden chopsticks.

"We did something normal," Elias said. "That was a lot of fun. It's been a while since I've done anything fun." He peeled the paper wrapping from his dessert, holding the slice of cheesecake delicately in his hand. "I feel guilty, kind of. Like I don't deserve to have a night like that."

Aarya gave him a knowing look, but didn't speak until Elias had finished his dessert and was lying back on the stone. "You wolfed it," she said. "I'm still trying to put the wasabi and ginger slices on mine."

"Take your time."

"Do you want one?"

"No, I don't want one of your seaweed things. They smell like a polluted lake."

"They do not." Aarya set the chopsticks down and pulled out her music player. "Do you want to listen?"

"If you insist."

"I don't insist, but let me find a good track." She fiddled with the player and held one of the ear buds close to her ear, and then extended it to Elias. "Here. Tell me if you like this one."

"Check for ear wax."

"It's fine. I wouldn't dare give it to you if it wasn't."

Elias stared up at the starry, moonlit sky as he listened. The tune harped on a theme of surrender and unity; it was gentle, lilting—characteristic of many of her favorites, he realized, or at least characteristic of the songs she shared with him.

Aarya stuffed the last roll into her mouth as the song ended. She tossed the chopsticks into the empty package and pulled one of the buds from Elias' ear. "Do you like it?" she asked. "I thought it might be too girly for you."

"I like it," he replied.

She stretched out beside him. "Remember, I chose these songs intentionally."

"And what is it you want us to surrender to?"

She smiled and didn't answer.

"I thought your playlists would have Buddhist chants and singing bowls and whatnot," Elias said.

"There are a few songs like that. In the 'Kinda happy' list. You can listen to them . . . whenever you're ready." Aarya pulled out her phone and checked the display. "The park is closing. Let's go."

"It doesn't actually close. No one's going to lock us in."

She looked at him with feigned exasperation. "True, but there's a communal agreement in place, and it's there for a reason." She stood up, taking her sushi package and Elias' cheesecake wrapper. "I can't hang out tomorrow. I'm working at the monastery. We have a fundraiser for one of our global relief programs in the morning. You can come to it, if you want. It's twenty dollars for breakfast, and the nuns are going to talk about the program and how it relates to Buddhist teachings—and in the evening, we have another prayer ceremony. Even if you show up late, you can come in and sit by the wall, like we did last time. I'll be there, and Beth will be there too."

Elias thought back to his emotional outburst in the prayer room, his pathetic sobs and dripping nose. "I'll think about it," he said.

And he did think about it, but he didn't show up to either event. He wasn't ready yet.

9

While Aarya ended her day on a positive note, Elias' night had just begun. He walked into the Woodlands Business Center and was greeted by Bruno's off-key singing. The werewolf had no gift for song; he believed that volume was the one ingredient that made singing great, and so Elias went into the kitchen and was blasted by Bruno's near-screaming rendition of "Hawaiian Sunset." The werewolf was rummaging in the refrigerator, his bottom swaying back and forth in time as he shouted about island sunsets.

Elias stuck his head into the kitchen. He was about to speak, but the werewolf belted again, this time about the sunrise.

"Bruno, please shut up," Elias implored him.

"Well, look who's back." Bruno straightened up, holding a package of sliced turkey in one hand and linked sausages in the other. "Oh, look who finally got rid of his girly haircut! Well, kind of. You traded it in for the boy band look. I was wondering where you run off to. Wasn't sure if you'd be back. I left you some coffee, though."

"Thank you. I appreciate it."

"Where else have you been?" The werewolf tore the plastic case from the sausages, first piercing it with his teeth, then peeling it away with his yellow fingernails. "You were gone a long time. Looking for a vivacious twenty-year-old to sink your teeth into?"

"No."

"Hanging around the nunnery with your new friend?"

Elias paused at the cupboard, his hand half-raised toward the coffee mugs.

"That's right," Bruno said. "We've seen you with your vampire pal. A wolf among sheep, isn't she? Clever. Don't know if I could pull it off, but good on her." He glanced back at Elias. "Or didn't she turn?"

"Are you following us?" Elias turned to face him, trying not to show his anxiety.

"You have a problem? Following is our game."

Elias nodded. He spoke in an emotionless tone. "Exactly. Following is our game. Being followed is not. I rather dislike it."

Bruno shrugged. He cradled the meat packages in one hand and pulled a beer from the fridge with the other. "And I dislike your high and mighty attitude, but I live with it. I guess some of the things we do just can't be helped."

He left the kitchen with his meal. Elias stood and listened to the retreating sounds of his footsteps.

The house was relatively quiet after Bruno went into his room. Slowly, Elias went about the task of pouring coffee and finding something to eat. The mini cheesecake had done nothing to sate his hunger, but Bruno had already ransacked the fridge, leaving it nearly empty except for condiments and beer. Elias settled for a sandwich with peanut butter and strawberry jam. It seemed a crude meal, but so did any meal he could have imagined at the moment. Once again, the task of chewing and digesting food seemed tedious and gross. The thought of it irritated him, making his movements rough and clumsy as he bustled around the kitchen.

He realized, though, that it was not the idea of food that disturbed him. Rather, it was Bruno's revelation. He knew about Aarya. Perhaps he didn't know everything, but he knew a little, and the little he knew might put her in danger.

Leitha came into the kitchen. She saw Elias and stopped, placing her hands on either side of the entryway. "Vlad," she said coyly, and laughed. "Look at you! Trying to get someone's attention?"

"Hello, Leitha," he replied gruffly.

She sidled up beside him. Elias deliberately turned away, spreading jam across the bread with rough strokes of the knife.

"You look good," she said. "But then, you always did."

He ignored her.

"You seem a bit tense," she added.

"I'm in a mood, Leitha. Don't bother me."

"What kind of mood, love? Can I make it better?"

"Yes, by going away," he replied.

Leitha leaned on the counter beside him, trying to get into his field of vision. "Maybe you can go away with me this time. We could go far, or near . . . very near, even just down the hall. There's a soft, cool spot on my bed that could use a bit of heating up."

"Leitha, you need to get lost."

"I can get lost with you, sweets. It's something I dream about." She reached out, running the backs of her fingers along his arm. "I could melt some of that—"

Elias turned on her, fangs bared, eyes burning with rage. Leitha backed away, her face full of sudden terror as he advanced on her.

"I am not sweet," he hissed, his angry face only inches from hers. "This is what I am. Is this what you want?" Elias grabbed Leitha's arms, felt his fingernails digging into her flesh.

"Elias, stop!" she cried.

"That's right: My name is Elias, and if you ever call me Vlad again, I'll chew your dim-witted head off. That's what I am, Leitha, and it's all you can ever expect as long as you keep surrounding yourself with monsters." He released her, taking a step back, his face still set in a threatening snarl. He took a few breaths, and added in a slightly calmer tone: "Do you know what I do to women like you? I seduce them, and I drain them, and I ruin them, and they go home and die. Is that what you want?"

Leitha had backed up into the corner. She began to slide sideways against the wall, inching toward the entryway, keeping her eyes on Elias. "That's not all you do," she retorted. "I know about you and your nun friend."

"Oh, you know about her too," he said. "Great. I'm being stalked."

"I guess she must be better than everyone else—not dim-witted like me."

Elias watched her go, and then returned to the task of making a sandwich. He tried to spread a slab of peanut butter onto the bread, but his violent movements only sent the knife piercing through the center. Elias stared at it. Then he threw the sandwich into the trash.

In the hall he nearly collided with Dayna. She didn't seem to be going anywhere in particular, but just stood in the hallway, silent and still—but when Elias jumped back, startled by her unexpected presence, she gave him a cold smile.

"Dayna," he said, trying to seem unruffled. "Hi."

The wendigo stared at him, and Elias suddenly realized what it was about her eyes that made them so strange. Not only did they never show any hint of feeling, but her pupils never changed; they never contracted, but stayed in the same dilated state, as though they were always starved for light. The rest of Dayna's physique gave off the same impression: she was pale, skinny, hollow-looking, with bony limbs and a wide but gaunt

103

face. On the rare occasions when Elias stood close to her (which, like tonight, only happened by accident), he felt a chill in the air around her, the same as if he was standing beside a leaky freezer.

Dayna raised her chin. Her hair fell away from her face, giving Elias a clearer view of her wide mouth—but her cold, unblinking eyes never moved from his face. In a low voice, she asked: "What is it?"

"What's what?"

He heard her inhaling, a rasping sound that was less like breathing and more like sandpaper against wood.

Elias waited. Dayna didn't respond, but only stared at him.

"Okay," he said, resisting a shudder. "Have a good night, then. See you around."

He retreated down the hall. Halfway to his rooms he looked back. Dayna hadn't moved, but stood there watching him. Her long, curved mouth, which usually bore the impression of a feigned smile, now seemed unsmiling and grim. It simply looked like the means of satisfying a ravenous hunger.

Elias spent the rest of the night shut up in his office, only going out for the restroom and a snack, and to spray air freshener around Dayna's rooms. On his trip to the bathroom, he'd noticed it even from far away: the vague smell of death, the rotting, foul scent that the wendigo could never quite cover with her perfumes. Elias kept bottles of freshener in the men's bathroom for the sole purpose of trying to chase away the smell she created.

At last he slept, and then made ready to endure another night at home. That night passed in much the same way; Elias did some cleaning around the business complex, and then tried his best to avoid his housemates. He woke early and crept outside, where he was delighted to find a package addressed to him. He snuck the parcel into his office and opened it. Inside was an antique brass padlock with green patina. Elias studied it for a while, tested the key to make sure it worked, and hid the padlock in a desk drawer.

Once he had his coffee and a light breakfast, Elias shut himself in his office and tried to focus on his work. His mind returned again and again to Aarya; everything leading up to his time with her was just an obligatory maneuver to ensure his survival. He finished his editing, looked at apartment listings, and listened to music. Elias had begun to familiarize himself with some of the songs, and found himself occasionally singing along. When he'd finished his work, he leaned back into his desk chair and closed his eyes, murmuring along with the lyrics, quietly singing about a sense of belonging with a treasured love.

The headphones were suddenly yanked from his head.

"What's this?" Bruno's voice asked.

Elias turned to see the werewolf standing with the headphones in hand, holding them over his ears with a perplexed scowl. "What is this pansy shit you're listening to?"

Elias stood up and grabbed the headset away from him. "This pansy shit is helping me relax. What the hell are you doing in my office?"

"I knocked, dufus, but you couldn't hear me over this lame drivel."

"So what do you want?"

Bruno shoved a slip of paper at him. "My rent check."

"Thank you." Elias took the check from him and placed it on the desk. "Is that all?"

"That will be all, sir," Bruno replied. "You may return to your pansy music."

Elias replaced the set on his own head and sat down again, leaning back into the cushioned leather. "You're one to talk, with your stockpile of luau songs. What kind of werewolf drools over the ukelele?"

Through the sound of delicate guitar and soft singing, Elias heard the werewolf say "To each his own."

The song switched. Two men's voices took turns at "A Change is Gonna Come," and then a women's choir began an angelic rendition of "The Blower's Daughter." Elias kept his eyes closed as he listened, trying to shut out the thoughts of his housemates, of the possibly kidnapped child—the almost certainly kidnapped child—and the weight of his situation in general. He felt his eyes becoming sore as the music coursed through him; he opened them and blinked, and realized with a shock that his eyes were tearing up with emotion. The music was perhaps too much. This household was not one in which it was safe to be vulnerable.

Elias switched the music off and went to the lab for another round of research. After reading through many of the lab's materials and doing tests on his own specimen samples, he'd felt ready to begin examining others. A discreet trip into the ladies' bathroom had gotten him a swab of Leitha's toothbrush, and he had retrieved samples from Luka and Bruno in a similar way, though the method for the werewolf was more repugnant: Bruno's toothbrush was cluttered with bits of food, but Elias had gotten a good sample by swabbing up some of the spittle he'd left in the sink.

The idea of getting a sample from Dayna was too unsettling. Elias wasn't sure he wanted to study her.

At some point, the smells from the kitchen drew his attention. His hunger was still unsated, so he followed the scents of cooked eggs and burnt toast, even the sour smell of fried bacon, and was surprised to find all of his roommates gathered in the kitchen. Leitha and Luka sat beside each other at the table; Dayna was there, too, and Bruno was moving between the stove and the table, dropping crisp slices of bacon onto the dining plates.

Elias stopped uncertainly, surveying the scene. After a moment he went to the fridge. He grabbed a carton of strawberries and started to leave.

Bruno scoffed at him. "Is that all you're having? No wonder you've got skin like Snow White and no more muscle than a noodle. Have a seat, have some protein. I feel like cooking. Do you want eggs?"

Elias glanced at the table. He wanted to decline, but after his confrontations with his housemates, he felt a need to appease them. "Sure," he said.

He sat at the far end of the table, across from Dayna. Bruno set a large serving of scrambled eggs in front of him. Though everyone at the table had plates heaped with food, no one ate. Dayna stared at Luka with her lizard-like eyes; Luka pushed his eggs and bacon back and forth across his plate; Leitha set her fork down, throwing sullen looks in Elias' direction.

Bruno threw several strips of bacon onto a sizzling pan, separating them with pair of tongs. He glanced back at the others. "Well, the gang's all here. Look at us, gathered around the table like a big, happy family."

"Luka doesn't like his food," Leitha said. "Isn't there something else he can have?"

"He'll eat that or nothing. I'm not cooking three special meals a day for him. Kid's getting to be too much of a bother."

Dayna's eyes flicked momentarily to Bruno; then she focused again on Luka. "I like kids," she said huskily, her lips barely moving as she spoke. "If you get tired of him, I'll take him off your hands."

Leitha gasped. "No! I got first dibs on Luka. He's mine." She reached a protective hand around his shoulders. "When he gets a little bit bigger, he can be my work mate. I'll teach him to be the smoothest pickpocket.

All these rich folks walking up and down main street could stand to lose a few pounds from their purses. And then I'll take him to the city, and he can hide under the tables and rip off of the fellows who are clubbing around and looking for tarts."

Elias sat with his fork halfway to his mouth, looking at Leitha with incredulity and distaste.

"What the hell are you grimacing at?" Bruno asked him. "Worthless goody two-shoes." He tossed a few pieces of bacon onto Elias' plate.

"I don't eat bacon," Elias said. He deposited the strips onto a napkin, wiping his fingertips on the corner.

"Why not? Too lowbrow for your tastes?"

"It smells like armpit."

Bruno snickered as he turned back to the stove. He set the spatula down and began to scratch himself, first under his chin, where he had missed several patches during his last shave—or perhaps those patches had simply grown out already. Bruno seemed to get hairier as the full moon approached. His eyebrows began to stand on end, and his scraggly patches of beard gave him a wild look. Bruno also had less patience for the task of bathing in the nights preceding the full moon. His odor was modest at the moment, but his skin had already begun to itch. The werewolf stood with his arms akimbo as he scratched his sides—rather like a monkey, Elias thought—and then he raised both hands to his head, digging his fingertips into his scalp with quick, erratic movements.

Elias put his fork down. "Could you please not do that, Bruno, for heaven's sake, just take a shower."

"Mind your beeswax," Bruno replied. The toaster sprung up, ejecting two slices of slightly charred bread. Bruno slathered them with grape jam and dropped them onto a plate already laden with toast. He turned to the table and stuffed the topmost piece into his mouth, taking a large bite and sending crumbles cascading onto the slices below. "Here you go, mate," he said, using his index finger to flick a couple of slices onto Elias' plate. "Just how you like it."

Elias stared at the crumbles that had scattered across the layer of jam. "Yes, there's nothing like toast with Bruno's mouth droppings in it."

Leitha restrained a laugh; then she remembered Elias' offense against her, and she quickly set her face back into a pout.

"Eat up," Bruno said. "Maybe if you had a bit of me in you, you wouldn't have that pansy smell." The werewolf leaned toward Elias and took a couple of loud sniffs. "It's getting worse."

"It's called shower gel," Elias replied.

"Shower gel doesn't stink like wimpling. The rest of you smell it, don't you?" Bruno went to stand beside Dayna, crouching to match the level of her gaze as he looked across the table at Elias. "Dayna, did you notice our roommate's new haircut? What do you think of it?"

The wendigo stared at Elias. Her eyes were flat and cold, yet Elias detected a glint of greed in them.

"Maybe the hairdresser left her scent on you, and it's clinging on for some reason. I suppose you smiled at her and thanked her, and maybe you gave her a big tip, and she went home happy that night. Did that affect you, Elias? Did you feel like you did a little bit of good for someone?"

"Let me do a bit of good for you, Bruno," Elias replied dryly. "Yes, I got my hair cut by a human, and I even went to the store and purchased soap and shampoo—and I didn't attack the hairdresser, or the cashiers, or the people stocking shelves. I went home and washed my hair in the shower, along with the rest of my body. It's called hygiene."

"Oh, that's a good story, but it doesn't explain why you look and smell like quarry. Is it just me?" Bruno looked from Dayna to Leitha. "It's not just me, is it? Our resident vampire is losing his edge. Must be all those trips to the nunnery with your little friend. Am I right? Is the nunnery the problem here?"

Dayna still stared at Elias. Her expression didn't change, but her lips parted suddenly, and for the first time Elias caught a glimpse of something behind those lips, a wide spread of something that gleamed in the kitchen light. For a moment it looked like her mouth was full of shiny plastic bits, but Elias quickly realized that he was seeing her teeth.

"Oh, no, he's still got his edge," Leitha said. "I'm not sure he's using it on humans, though."

Elias gave her a look and stood up, dumping the contents of his plate into the trash.

As he left the kitchen, Bruno called after him: "Just giving you a fair warning. Not that anyone would miss your snobbery if something did happen to you."

In the morning, Elias went to see Aarya. She had asked him to bring a small picnic, so he stopped to buy crackers, sliced cheese, and hummus. He brought a pair of coffee mugs and a thermos full of hot coffee and cream.

They met in the pre-dawn darkness, at the little park with the pathetic waterfall. Elias took a picnic cloth from the vinyl carrying case he'd brought; he spread the cloth across the flat rock in the middle of the grassy field, setting up the food in the middle.

"You thought of everything," Aarya said, placing a napkin and mug in front of Elias. "Except light. I can barely see. Do you trust me to pour your coffee?"

"No, but give it a try anyway."

She filled both mugs and set out two miniature paper

plates. Aarya was wearing the new jacket, and she had her hair styled in the same "messy" way that the hairdresser had suggested, but she quickly smashed it beneath a knit cap. "It's getting cold out again," she said. "I'm glad you brought hot coffee. In a little while, we'll have to start meeting indoors. I'm not a huge fan of the cold."

"Wherever you want," he replied.

When they had finished eating, they packed the wrappers and leftovers back into the case and sipped at the last of the coffee. "I have something for you," Aarya said, reaching into her jacket. She pulled out a small book and showed him the cover. "It's the Dhammapada, the sayings of the—"

"No, no." Elias held up his hands, palms out, as if to ward off the threat that the book posed to him. "I can't take that home with me."

Aarya slipped it back into her pocket. "I'll hang onto it. You can look through it when you come over."

"I don't want to go to your house again."

"What? Why not?"

Elias debated how to answer. If Aarya was in any danger, she should know—but he didn't want to scare her unnecessarily. Then again, Aarya wasn't one who scared easily, if at all. "My roommates have seen us together. Leitha must have followed me one night."

As usual, Aarya seemed unperturbed. "Is she dangerous?"

"No. She's annoying. But the fact that I'm hanging around you, and around the monastery . . . it gets on Bruno's nerves."

"Move out," she said.

"I will. I've been looking at places. I called a couple of them before I came over. One is having an open house in a couple of days; I have to get up at one-thirty to see it. I left a message for the other one."

111

"Good for you." Aarya set her empty mug on the stone beside her. She drew her knees up to her chest, hugging her arms around them to keep warm. "Doesn't it get boring, hanging around that building all night?" she asked. "I know you have a job, but it doesn't sound like there's much else going on. How else do you spend your time? Do you have hobbies, or . . . ."

"Not really. I did night photography for a little while, but . . . it wasn't very inspiring. I put the pictures into a stock photo account and made a few dollars, and that was the end of it. Why, what do you do besides running back and forth to the abbey? Do you even have a job?"

"I work at the library," Aarya said. "Entry-level stuff. Sorting books, stocking shelves. Do you still read?"

"Yes. Non-fiction only. Science, history. Things like that." Elias thought back over the repetitive nights he'd spent before meeting Aarya. "I do have a new hobby. In the building where I live, there's a health lab. They got rid of the patient records, but they left a lot of the equipment behind. I've been learning how to examine blood and saliva samples."

She gave him an incredulous look. "That's a hobby?"

"I'm learning how to read genetic markers. You started me off on that, actually."

"How?"

"By not becoming a vampire. I wanted to see if there was something in the blood that decides whether people turn or not. I'm already finding things out about my own DNA." He added casually: "You should let me give you a buccal swab."

"A what?" Aarya asked.

"A swab to the inside of your cheek. I can take it home and use it to study your DNA."

"No way, Elias, that's so weird."

"Fine," Elias said, "but you agreed that I should do

something good. Maybe this is my thing."

"How is that good? Even if people have a genetic trait that makes them more susceptible, how is knowing that going to make any difference? What can you do with it?"

"Gene therapy."

"And who's going to sponsor gene therapy for vampires? This isn't something that conventional medicine can heal, anyway. It wasn't caused by a physical disease."

"Neither is addiction," Elias replied, "but there's a genetic component to it."

She gave him a dubious look. "I'm not letting you swab me."

"Fine. I'll bring my swabs anyway, just in case you change your mind." Elias leaned over, grabbing Aarya's empty mug. He packed both of the mugs into the case and zipped it shut. "So, yes, living in the office building is boring, but it's more than that. It's dangerous and . . . it's vile. Especially now." Elias took a quiet breath, trying his best to make his voice sound casual. "When I move out . . . do you want to live with me? I know it might be too soon, but . . . maybe I'll rent a place that has enough space for both of us, in case you decide to join me. Not that you need much space, with your two pieces of furniture."

Aarya looked back at him in silence. He couldn't read her expression.

"I know I have a lot of red flags right now," Elias said, "but maybe in a few weeks, or a few months, you'll look at me and they won't be there anymore. If I ever act like a prick, you can lecture me, or punch me in the face, or whatever." He reached up, gingerly touching his nose. "You left me in a sorry situation, by the way, when you hit me. I can't go home to a place like mine and admit that someone punched me. I didn't have any water with me, but I had a tissue, and I had a bottle of windshield wiper fluid in my car. I had to use that to clean the blood off my face."

"Really," she replied softly. "How was that?"

"I don't recommend it. I thought I was going to be sick." Elias stood up and grabbed the case. "You look cold. Should we walk?"

"Sure."

The sun was close to emerging over the horizon as they walked toward the bridge. "After you hit me," Elias said, "I started to remember that pack of boys who used to run around your neighborhood. One of the first times I came to your house, we were just walking down the street, and one of them walked up to you and kicked the back of your leg, and called you a skank. Just out of the blue. And you turned around and sucker punched him— and he was sitting on the ground with this shocked look on his face, with blood dripping out of his nose. And then he got up and started screaming that he was going to kill you, and you punched him again." He looked sidelong at Aarya, saw her face calm and unruffled. "They're the ones who made you tough. Weren't they? I remember you were the only girl in the neighborhood, and they used to follow you around and harass you."

"Yeah."

"When you moved, were you glad to get out of there?"

She sighed. "I was glad to be rid of those particular boys, but I liked where I lived. I hated leaving."

"I thought that wherever you went must have been so much better, and that you were glad to leave this place in the dust." The grass ended below Elias' feet, giving way to the walking path. He kicked at a loose section of pavement. "How come you didn't write to me?"

"I did, Elias. I wrote letters, and I called. A man kept

114

answering the phone and saying I had the wrong number. It was probably your dad, and—"

"My stepdad. He changed our phone number."

"Why?"

"I don't know."

"I wrote, too. I never heard back, so after a while I quit."

"I never got a letter from you." Elias thought back to that time, but his mind refused to dredge up too much detail. "He might have taken them. He didn't want me getting close to anyone." Elias paused, and reluctantly said: "I've been having nightmares . . . ."

"About him?"

"Yeah." He looked at her again, saw a sympathetic understanding in her eyes. "You knew something was wrong about him. When you met him, I mean, you knew right away. He came to pick me up at your house, and you looked at him like . . . like you didn't trust him."

"*You* didn't trust him," Aarya said. "He came into the house, and you didn't look at him. You stared at the floor with a blank look on your face, like you had shut down. He was all smiles and friendliness, and he put his hand on your shoulder, and you froze. You were standing there like a statue, and he told you to say thanks to us, and you looked at me like . . . I don't know. Like you needed help. But you forced a smile and said thanks, and your eyes glazed over, and everything about it just looked wrong."

"Well, you were more perceptive than a lot of other people."

"How did you get away from him?" she asked.

"I planned it for years. All through high school I studied coding and web design, and got a copy editing certificate and did freelance work. When I was almost seventeen, I made an arrangement with a guy who was renting out his basement. He didn't want to sign me on because I was a minor, but I showed him my paychecks and agreed to pay his mortgage every month, so he let me stay. I warned my stepdad that if he sent anyone after me, I would tell everyone about him. And I never spoke to that slimy bastard again."

They had reached the center of the walking bridge. "Hang on," Elias said, and pulled the brass padlock from his pocket. "I know it's cheesy, but I got us a padlock."

Aarya looked up at him with an amused smile. "You got us a love lock?"

"It's not really love-themed—not in the romantic sense. It's Buddha-themed. I thought you would prefer it."

He held the lock up in his palm, allowing Aarya to study the details. In the contrast of polished and dirty brass, and the smattering of green patina, two figures were depicted side by side on the front of the lock: a four-armed deity and a human-like figure with an elephant head.

Aarya took the padlock from him. She scrutinized it with a serious expression, and then she laughed. "This is Hindu iconography, not Buddhist. The elephant is Ganesh. And I think the other one is . . . is it Vishnu?"

"You're asking me? I thought it was Buddha. Still, it's cool, isn't it?"

"Ganesh is actually appropriate for you, I think. And for me. Ganesh is a deity of new beginnings."

"What about the other one?"

"I don't know. I think Vishnu represents dharma."

"Which is . . . ?"

"Righteousness. Goodness. There isn't really a good translation for it."

"Well, then, it's a fitting symbolism for us. You already have a crucifix and a book of Buddhist guidance. Now you can add a Hindu padlock to the mix."

Aarya frowned as she studied the back of the lock.

"But, Elias, we can't write our names on this. It's too dark."

"Do we need names? We have our pictures. You can be the one that looks like a human, and I'll be the one with the elephant head. That fits, too, right? You're more about goodness than I am." Elias held out his hand. "Give it here. You can pick a good spot, and I'll lock it."

"No, wait," Aarya said. "We can't just stick it on there. There has to be some sort of ceremony around it. I'm sure all these other people professed their love, or made commitments, before they locked things in place."

Elias restrained a smile. "What would you like me to profess to you?" he asked.

"I want you to commit to being decent," she replied, giving him an almost challenging look. "Don't harm others. Can you promise that?"

He gave it serious thought. Elias wanted to say yes, but he felt glimmers of doubt as he remembered the way he'd snapped at Aarya, the way he'd snapped at Leitha. "I promise I will do my best."

"You already said that you want to be with me, and I want to be with you, too, but this is more important," Aarya said.

"What's more important? Being decent? Collecting good karma, so I can make it to the finish line?"

She gave him a mildly exasperated look. "You can't do things just to collect good karma for yourself. You have to do it from your heart, out of love for others. If you do it only for yourself, you add a drop of poison to every good deed."

Elias sighed. "You sound like a Buddhist manual."

She pointed at him, poking her finger into his chest. "Don't harm others," she said. "Perpetuate kindness instead."

"Fine. I commit," Elias relented. "I will perpetuate

kindness—until someone tries to make me into a doormat. I reserve the right to perpetuate self-defense, too."

"Good enough." Aarya handed him the lock. "And what would you like me to commit to?"

"Live with me, someday," Elias said.

She nodded. "Someday. Even if it's in a month, or even if it's as far off as nirvana—if you keep holding up your end of the bargain, we will live together."

Elias chuckled as he moved toward the fence. "Nirvana?" He held the padlock in an open spot among the locks. "What about right here?"

"Go for it."

He slid the metal bar through the fence and pushed it into the lock. "There we are," he said, stepping back. "Ours is the best one, don't you think?"

"There isn't a best one," she replied.

Elias looked down at her with open affection. "I meant what I said: I will try to do better in this life, and I'm grateful to you. Thank you for not cutting my head off, or siphoning all of my blood, or driving a stake through my heart." Elias nudged her and added: "You make some mean threats. It doesn't seem very consistent with your wanting to be like Christ and Buddha."

"I didn't say that I'm like them. I said that I admire them." She gave him a wily grin and started past him.

"Aarya," he said, placing a hand on her arm.

She turned to him, and he leaned down and kissed her—just for a moment, because Aarya drew her head back in surprise. A few love-scrawled padlocks clanged against the wire barrier as she bumped against them.

"Sorry," Elias said.

"No . . . it's fine. I was just surprised."

They stood looking at each other. Elias leaned forward and kissed her again, briefly. He drew her into a light embrace, sliding his hand behind her head, moving his lips close to Aarya's neck. As his mouth brushed against her skin, she gasped and pulled back again.

Elias lowered his arms, letting her withdraw. "I'm not going to harm you," he said.

Among the hushed breezes and distant chirping of night creatures, Elias heard Aarya's heart pounding. She took a few moments to catch her breath, looking intently into his eyes. "I know," she whispered.

Slowly, he bent to kiss her again. Elias hesitated for a moment with his lips close to her neck, sensing the delicateness of the flesh that lay between his mouth and Aarya's veins. He kissed her there, tenderly, feeling the wild heartbeat beneath her soft skin—and though his own heart was beating fast, in that moment Elias felt an unprecedented sensation of calm. The feeling of his lips against Aarya's flesh made a near lifetime of struggles and pains seem suddenly resolved: his fear of trusting another person, the ugliness he associated with being touched; the despairing expectation of endless, helpless loneliness and rage, and the desire to reveal his rage to the world. All the trials and nightmares of those years seemed to have culminated in that one resolute moment, in the contrast between what Elias could have chosen and what he chose instead.

Elias moved his lips farther down her neck, kissing her once more near her shoulder. Aarya's breathing changed. She began to make soft, shuddering sounds, and when Elias pulled away, he saw that she was crying.

"What's the matter?" he asked.

Aarya shook her head, sending tears spilling down her face.

Elias tried to read the look in her eyes. He saw grief there, and it dawned on him that she might be thinking about Zoua. Here she was having fun, even being intimate, with the person who had unwittingly helped cause Zoua's death. Aarya likely felt a sense of guilt, perhaps even shame. "Are you crying for me?" he asked. "Or are you thinking about your friend?"

She nodded and wiped at her face. "Zoua. I miss her. And I feel bad for her." She finished wiping her tears and looked up at Elias. "I'm not trying to make you feel guilty, not now. I just . . . ."

She trailed off. Elias said: "I'm really sorry. I don't know what else to say."

"You don't have to say anything. Just hug me." Aarya leaned into his arms and embraced him. "I'm not just sad," she said, resting her head against his chest. "I'm relieved."

They stood there, Aarya gazing at the early morning light reflecting off the metal and plastic locks and at the sparkling stream beyond, and Elias with his eyes closed, focusing on the rhythm of Aarya's pulse against his.

"We should go," he said finally, looking down at her. "The park isn't actually open yet, and I know how important it is for you to follow communal agreements. Right?"

She let out a soft laugh.

"Come on." Elias took her hand, and they walked together into the dawn.

10

Elias woke early that night and repeated his routine of making coffee, washing up, and grabbing a snack from the kitchen. He avoided his housemates for the first couple of hours, but when he emerged from his office for a bathroom trip, he found Dayna standing outside his door.

"Jesus," he gasped, recovering from the shock of seeing her there. "Hi, Dayna." His gaze fell to the paper in her hand. "Oh. Your rent check?"

She handed the slip of paper to him. Elias was about to close the door on her, but Dayna asked in a sharp voice: "What is it?"

He restrained a sigh. "What's what? You'll have to be more specific."

The wendigo's thin lips began to part, revealing a glimpse of a wide spread of teeth. For the first time, Elias saw Dayna's pupils move. They contracted ever so slightly, just enough to be noticeable. In a slow, raspy whisper, she said: "I want it."

Elias took a step back. He placed his hand on the door, ready to slam it shut if necessary. "You want what?"

He heard the slow heave of her breath, but she said nothing.

"Right. Well, this conversation seems like a fail, so I'm going to end it here. Goodnight." Elias closed the door. He stood with his foot braced against it, and with his hand clutching the knob, for several minutes.

The encounter rattled him. After he mustered enough

courage to make a bathroom run, Elias hurried back to the office and listened to Aarya's "Relax" playlist while he dusted the room and swept the floor. The music calmed him; song by song, it eased his sense of danger, until he was letting his voice rise and fall with the music: "Take my ego and my pain, baptize my soul in your—"

He startled as the bedroom door opened. Leitha stood there, her face devoid of its usual flirty grin. She stepped inside, closed the door, and gave Elias a serious once-over. "Are you getting baptized now? I can crochet you one of those little white baptism dresses."

Elias pulled the earphones out. "When did knocking go out of fashion?"

"I can hear your singing out in the hall."

"And?"

"And I thought you should know," she replied. "If Bruno hears it . . . he's already agitated about you."

"Seems like he's not the only one. Everyone's agitated these days." Elias looked her over, noting the contrast between her sparkly "Ready for bliss" T-shirt and the unhappiness written in her face. "I appreciate the warning, Leitha," he said. "And I've been wanting to apologize to you. I should have done it earlier. I'm sorry I yelled at you that night, and that I grabbed you. I really am. But I'm establishing a boundary here: Do not flirt with me."

"All right," she replied quietly. "I probably deserved it anyway. I'm the one who told Bruno about your nun friend." She leaned back against the door, watching Elias with somber eyes. "She's not a monster at all, is she?"

Elias placed the music player in his desk. "She's not a nun," he replied vaguely.

"I followed you," Leitha said. "I didn't mean anything by it. I just liked you." Elias still didn't respond, so she asked: "Are you in love?"

It seemed a dangerous question to answer, but Elias

was honest anyway. "Yes," he admitted.

"It looks good on you." Leitha smiled—a minuscule, sad sort of smile. "Is she safe, though? Isn't she the crazy woman who came running through here?"

"She's as safe as it gets."

Leitha came toward him, daring to touch a lock of his hair. "Was this her idea?"

"Sort of."

"Be careful with people like that. She should take you as you are."

"No one should take a vampire as he is. Anyway, I'm the one who told her to change her hair first. I made her change her wardrobe, too."

"Well, after seeing her, I don't blame you." Another faint smile touched Leitha's lips. "Is it true you're leaving us? Bruno thinks you are."

Elias debated how to answer her. "I don't know yet. Things are complicated. If I do, I won't just leave you hanging. Okay? We'll work on your coding, and get you set up, and we'll get you another housemate. One who isn't too . . . unsavory."

Leitha was nodding, slowly. "I believe you. You're a good one, Elias."

He started to reply, but Leitha turned and left the room.

It was around one o'clock that the business complex received a visitor. Elias went to the kitchen, looking for lunch, and found Bruno once again at the stove with pans of sizzling bacon and some other dish that looked like a mash-up of ground hamburger and beans. Bruno's persistent presence in the kitchen didn't surprise him. The werewolf was ravenous at this time of the month, and tried to sate his growing hunger with near-constant meals and nightly trips to the grocery store.

The strategy wouldn't last, though. Bruno's cravings

had a restless anger behind them, an anger that would wriggle and nag inside of him until it drove him out into the streets, where unknowing humans emerged, ready for the nightlife or returning from late engagements. Lashing out at such people was the only way to satisfy Bruno's anger—but it was a counterfeit satisfaction, and it never lasted.

"Well, well," Bruno said as Elias stepped inside. "Look who's joining us for lunch."

Elias glanced at the table, expecting to see Luka, but someone else sat in the boy's place: a woman, tall and pale, dressed in a high-neck coat and leather gloves. Her flesh had gray-blue undertones, the same shade that stained the whites of her eyes, and her lowered eyelids were red-rimmed, such a deep red that Elias at first thought she was bleeding. Despite her weary appearance, it was evident that she was young. The woman saw Elias looking at her and dipped her head, obscuring her face with her long hair—a common reflex of monsters.

"And who do we have here?" Elias asked.

"That's Annis."

"Annis," Elias repeated, his gaze still locked on the woman. "What brings you here, Annis?"

Slowly, she stood up from the table. The woman's dark blond hair still veiled her face, but Elias could see her peering at him with her one visible eye. "Real estate," she replied in a raspy voice. "But right now I just need the restroom."

"In the front," Bruno replied, "by the doors."

She stood up and moved toward the hall. Her coat hung open, and beneath it Elias could see her clothes: a tank top and leggings under a leather skirt. On her chest, two talismans hung from leather cording. The skirt was stitched together with contrasting shades of beige and brown, cinched at the waist with a scrappy-looking

124

leather belt.

He waited until he heard the restroom door closing behind her. "What the hell is she doing here?" he asked Bruno.

"Looking for a place to live."

"So . . . ." Elias paused as Bruno's words began to sink in. "You mean she wants to live *here*."

Bruno gave him a knowing smirk. "Well, someone's got to move in, am I right? I saw the printout in your office with the cozy little apartment listings. Some real nice properties out on the other side of town. Two-bedroom townhouse, upper level, three-season porch, outdoor swimming pool and hot tub . . . ."

Elias unclenched his teeth and asked: "Why the hell were you in my office?"

"You knew I was there, dimwit. I was standing right behind you while you were listening to that tansy-pansy crap. Your dream-home listings were sitting on your printer."

Elias took a few breaths, trying to ease his sudden anxiety. "Regardless of whatever kind of printout I had in my office, we don't just let random strangers into this building. We have a vote first."

"Says you, but your say doesn't count if you're leaving." Bruno grabbed a short strip of bacon from the plate and popped it into his mouth.

"It's true, I might leave," Elias replied. "But I won't just take off. You'll have plenty of notice, and plenty of time to find another roommate."

"Sure, sure. I'm supposed to take your word for it, am I? I don't know about that. You're full of surprises lately."

As Elias pondered what to say next, he became aware of the silence in the front lobby. The restrooms were just across from the main doors, between the kitchen and TV room. Even though Elias had sharp hearing, he no longer heard Annis' movements. He stepped out into the hall, listening, and glanced back at Bruno. "Didn't she say she was going to use the bathroom?"

"Yeah, so what?"

Elias listened again. He thought back to Annis' clothes, to her long, gloved fingers and leather skirts. "Where is Luka?"

"Sleeping."

"Does she know that you have a son?"

"Maybe. What about it?"

Elias turned and walked briskly toward Bruno's part of the complex, toward the room where Luka slept on a foldout cot. He threw open the door, and the light from the hall fell directly on the sleeping boy. Annis couched beside him, half on the cot, her knee pressed close beside Luka, her hands poised above his throat. The creature's gloves had been cast onto the floor, revealing pale hands and bony fingers—and on each index finger, a long, curved talon that came to a deadly point.

She turned her head, looking at Elias with fiery eyes. He leapt before she had time to react. Annis was hurled from the cot and onto the floor. A dull cracking sounded as her skull smacked the linoleum.

Elias grabbed her wrists and brought one of her hands close to her face, so that the points of her claws trembled a mere inch from her eye. The monster stopped moving; the fire receded from her gaze.

"If you ever try to touch that boy again," Elias said in a loud whisper, "I will skin you myself. I will rip out your claws and use them to cut you open, and I will take enough skin to make up for every inch of flesh you've stolen, even if I have to skin all of your organs and every last bit of your intestines."

She snarled and thrashed, with no effect. In a moment, though, Annis thrashed more violently, throwing Elias

126

aside and leaving a gash along his forearm. She sneered at him and fled from the room.

Luka was just beginning to stir from sleep. As Elias stood, examining the fresh wound on his arm, the boy rubbed his eyes and looked up at him.

Elias covered the wound with his hand. "Sorry, Luka," he said. "I didn't mean to wake you. Go back to sleep, okay?"

The boy looked at him with drowsy eyes.

Bruno's heavy footfalls sounded in the hallway. Elias stepped out and closed the door, putting a hand to his lips as Bruno began to shout at him: "What the hell? Annis just ran out the front. What'd you do?"

Elias moved toward him, stopping him further down the hall. His voice was a quiet, angry hiss. "That thing just tried to kill your son."

Bruno looked genuinely befuddled. "What?"

"You heard me. She's a skinner. She was about to slice Luka open with her two-inch-long claws." Elias showed him the gash on his arm. "This is exactly why we don't let just anyone through those doors."

"Calm down," Bruno said. "It's just a scratch. And Luka's fine; it's good for him to tussle with monsters. By the time he's grown, he'll know how to deal with our lot."

The door opened behind Elias. He looked back and saw Luka coming into the hall, dressed in one of Leitha's T-shirts.

Elias went to him and picked him up. "Are you all right?" he asked. The boy didn't look frightened; he didn't seem to realize what had happened. Elias looked down and saw that he had smeared the boy's shirt with blood. "It's bedtime, okay? Let's get you tucked in."

Bruno grabbed Elias' shoulder. "Give him here. You think you're his dad now? I got him." He pulled the child out of Elias' arms. "Come on boy, back to your room.

Dad's got important things to do."

Elias watched them go. Luka peered at him over Bruno's shoulder, his large brown eyes full of tranquil obliviousness. Elias' arms, which had pinned Annis only a minutes ago, suddenly felt useless. Taking Luka somewhere safe was not an option, not as long as Bruno was around. Perhaps all Elias needed to do was wait for a moment when Bruno was otherwise occupied—but when would that moment be? If Elias stayed for another month or two, he wouldn't be able to take Luka with him when he left. The boy wouldn't survive that long.

Unsettled and desperate, Elias went for his coat. He would ask for guidance from Aarya. She was wise; she would have advice, maybe even a solution.

He stopped in the bathroom to clean his wound and bandage it. He would have to remember to keep the coat on; he didn't want Aarya to know he was hurt.

As he drove toward downtown, Elias looked repeatedly in the rearview mirror, looking for another car trailing him, or for dark figures pursuing him in the shadows. He saw nothing and decided he had little to fear at the moment. Leitha wouldn't follow him again, and Annis was likely long gone.

Beth's house was dark. Elias knocked and rang the bell a few times before giving up and heading for the monastery. He hoped to see Beth's car in the lot, or Aarya's rusty red Chevy, but found neither of them on his arrival. He parked anyway and headed for the buildings.

The windows of the left-hand cabin still glowed with light. Elias quickened his pace as he cut across the middle of the stone courtyard, hurrying down the two short steps and through the plaza. He had almost reached the dollar-store Buddha when saw a pair of bright eyes staring at him in the moonlight, just a few feet ahead of him; a figure sat there on the courtyard wall, quietly awaiting his

128

approach.

Elias jumped back, struggling to keep his balance, his eyes locked on the figure in front of him. The woman bore the scent of a human (not Annis, he realized with relief). She was dressed in a knit cap and a pair of yellow and dark red robes.

"Hi," the woman said. Elias recognized her as one of the nuns from the prayer ceremony: the oldest-looking woman with a deeply lined face, the one with dark eyes and tanned skin—the least potato-like of the group, he'd thought.

Elias bent forward, placing his hands on his knees. "You scared me," he said breathlessly. He closed his eyes, trying to calm his racing heart.

"Sorry about that."

"I'm looking for Aarya and Beth."

"You just missed them," she said.

Elias slowly straightened up. The nun asked: "Is everything okay?"

"No," he said. "Not really. I need help."

The nun watched him for a moment, then stood up and beckoned him. "Come inside."

She led him not to the dormitory, but to the right-hand cabin and the prayer room. She turned on a single overhead light, and then went to the table at the far end and lit several tea candles. Without turning around, she gestured to the floor. "Sit down," she said.

Elias sat at the place she indicated, at the edge of the deep red oriental rug. As he tried to shift into a comfortable position in this space where nuns had prayed, Elias was overcome by a sense of not belonging—of committing some sort of blasphemous intrusion.

"Um . . . Ms. . . . I don't know your name," he said.

"Lamia," she replied. "And you're Elias."

He resisted a chuckle, but couldn't help saying aloud:

"Lamia, like the demon?"

"Yes," she replied. "Just like the demon. A worse demon than you, even." She turned and sat down at the edge of the rug, across from Elias. As he looked into her bright, dark eyes, he had a sudden impression of someone with an almost unimaginable vastness of experience—an old, intelligent creature who had lived a thousand years in one lifetime, and many lifetimes before that.

"Did Aarya tell you about me?" Lamia asked.

Elias hesitated. "She might have. She said that there was a nun who used to be . . . like me."

Lamia nodded. "And now you know my name. Maybe you can guess what kind of crimes I committed."

Lamia's legend was old and infamous; Elias knew her as a vengeful demon who preyed on children. She must have known that he knew, yet she regarded him with guiltless calm.

"You said you needed help," Lamia reminded him. "What exactly is it that you need?"

"I don't know. I'm just . . . in a difficult spot. My housemates found out that I've been spending time here, and they're not happy about it. I'm worried that they're going to target the monastery. And Aarya. I think I'm putting her in danger."

The nun seemed unconcerned. She looked down at the rug, her eyes moving over the black and silver patterns along the edges. "Monsters don't like seeing others return to being human," she said at last. "They detest the idea of humanness. I'm sure you know that already." She glanced up at Elias. "When they see it, it challenges their belief that monstrosity is impossible to heal. Monsters like to act invulnerable, but they're terrified of facing themselves. When they see someone like you doing it, it provokes something in them that they would rather not face."

"Whatever the reason," Elias said, "they're pissed

off."

"You don't have to stay there," Lamia replied. "If the issue is that you have nowhere to go, we can find a place for you. Somewhere you'll be safe. As for the monastery, don't worry about us. We can defend ourselves."

"It's more complicated than that," Elias said. "My housemate, Bruno . . . he's a big guy. He gets wild during the full moon."

Lamia nodded. "Right about now. That's why I was outside tonight: full moon, clear sky. When you're in bed every night at ten o'clock, there are times when you miss the night."

"He kidnapped a boy," Elias said. "I assume it's a kidnapping. The boy is Bruno's biological son. He brought him home one day and said he was going to raise him to be one of us. But he's getting tired of taking care of him, and . . . it's not safe for a child in a place like that."

"And you care about this boy," Lamia said.

Elias hesitated, thrown off by the comment, even vaguely suspicious of her intentions. Was it true that she had preyed on children? And if so, how could he trust her? Lamia, in legend, had preyed on kids to get revenge; she had lost her own children to violence, and in a heartbroken madness had found a way to force her pain on others.

"Since when do you care about the fate of a human?" Lamia paused, and continued to press Elias: "Does he remind you of yourself when you were young?"

He thought back to his own youth, but the effort was stunted, as usual. He supposed that he was sensitive to the idea of a child being abused, but at the same time, Elias saw no reflection of himself when he looked at Luka. He merely saw a boy who didn't deserve to be hurt, and grown-ups who were capable of little else. "Did Aarya tell you about my childhood?" he asked.

"She did. Does that bother you?"

He hesitated. "A week ago, it would have. But I just don't care anymore. It . . . doesn't seem to mean anything."

"You can take the boy to the police," Lamia said.

"I can't, actually," Elias said. "Bruno would let someone skin that boy right in front of him, but he would never let me take him out of the house. He thinks of this boy as his property. And if the police showed up, they wouldn't stand a chance. He would rip them to shreds and run."

"Who else lives there?"

"A succubus, sort of. And a wendigo."

The nun's brow twitched. "A wendigo? Are you sure?"

"Well . . . that's what Bruno said she was."

"It's not likely," Lamia said. "Wendigos can't live with others. They have no restraint, and no desire to cooperate. They're consumed by their hunger."

"Hunger for what?" Elias asked. "I've never actually seen her eat."

"A wendigo perceives things like love, happiness, and hope as the richest foods. They crave those things with obsessive desperation, and when they find them, they devour them. They try to devour the soul that is happy, vibrant, and full of hope—but wendigos don't know how to create those feelings themselves, and so they are never sated."

Lamia stood up and went to the table. She crouched there, reaching beneath the draping cloth and pulling a few boxes from beneath—cardboard boxes, mostly, and then one polished wooden box, small and rectangular. She seated herself in front of Elias again and set the box on the rug.

"You know that in Vinaya, one of the teachings is to refrain from harming others," she said.

"Yes. Well, I know that's a Buddhist teaching."

"In the time you've been here, have you seen any weapons?"

"No," Elias said, and couldn't help thinking: *Just a lot of bald women and cheap decor.* "But I suppose you could have a stockpile hidden away somewhere."

"Instead of weapons, we have healing instruments," Lamia said. "To some, though, like your roommates, a healing instrument is a weapon—a potentially fatal one, because they see themselves as evil, and it aims to destroy the parts of them that are evil. It targets the darkness in them and casts everything in light, and exposes the things that they would rather not see." Lamia opened the case and pulled out a thick red cloth, unfolding it in her lap. "Healing is sometimes the most terrifying specter. It carries with it a necessary confrontation with everything else that you fear." She pulled an object from the folds of cloth: a small knife with a carved wooden handle.

"It's an astra blade," she said, extending it to him. "Made of materials from another dimension, but bound by the arts to this one."

Elias took it and pulled the knife from its sheath. The small, silver blade was remarkably dull, too dull to cut anything. Elias didn't find it particularly terrifying.

"Another dimension?" he asked. "And how do you happen to have it?"

Lamia chuckled. "Well, that's a long story—a story for another time."

"What does it do?"

"It cuts," she said. "It's sharper than it looks. Try piercing your hand with it—just a little poke."

Elias looked up at her. The nun had a certain glimmer in her eye, a trace of something like amusement, or

133

perhaps just expectation.

He turned the knife in his hand. As he moved, the blade reflected the multitude of flickering candle flames, so much so that it seemed to produce its own light. Elias gripped the handle and brought the edge of the blade close to his palm, but stopped at the feeling of a strange vibration, a silent hum that seemed to come from the metal. He shifted the knife in his hand, bringing the tip close to his flesh, and gave himself a small poke.

A shock coursed through him—an almost painful burst of warmth that seemed to crack his bones and tear pieces of his insides. Elias gasped and dropped the knife, letting it fall into his lap.

Slowly, he lifted his arm and stared at his hand. The blade had left no mark, and Elias was not in any pain; he only felt a slight soreness in his chest, the same he'd felt on the night of the prayer ceremony.

"The purpose of the astra is to cut the toughest of shells that will not break through prayer, or through manipulating chi, or other conventional means," Lamia said. "If you need to use it to defend yourself, use it on bare skin. Don't try to push it through people's clothes; it may not work. But remember that the shock of the astra, for many people—and especially for people who have become monsters—is so great that they can't endure it."

"So, what happens to them?" Elias asked, carefully placing the knife back in its sheath.

"The astra pierces the veil around the soul. If one has too little command of one's soul, it flees into the afterlife."

"You mean, it kills them," Elias said.

Lamia nodded. "It might. It may just shock them."

"And yet, you just asked me to stab myself with it."

The nun gave him a somber smile. "You're taking a very slow path toward redemption, Elias, and that's the way most people have to take it: slowly. People chip away at the shell they've created around their souls, and then they get scared, or discouraged, and they cover it up again, and sometimes they even stop for a while, but all the while they're still working their way out of that darkness. And I know you're uncertain about whether you can make it out, but I see the difference in you already. You're not in so deep that the astra would harm you."

Elias lowered his eyes, his own doubt nagging at him.

"And remember," she added, "if you need a place to go, you can come here—at any hour. Knock at the door on the other building, and I will open it for you."

"Why?" Elias asked. "I might have dangerous people coming after me. If you're unarmed, why invite monsters here?"

She shrugged. "What else would we do?"

"I don't know. Send me to the police?"

"Go to them, too, but they won't shelter you." Lamia gave him a grave look. "I've harmed others in my past, and I've even taken a life," she said, with a subtle note of grief. "More than one—in another lifetime, maybe, but not that long ago. What can I do now, except protect others, and especially children?"

"You believe in reincarnation," Elias said, catching her meaning. "These crimes you committed—you think you committed them in a past life."

"Perhaps," she said, and once again Elias saw the impression of immense age in the woman's aura. "Or perhaps I've just had one long life, trapped at one age, with no death and birth in between."

Elias shifted, making ready to stand and leave. He found himself suddenly daunted by the intensity of Lamia's gaze.

"Do you know what death, birth, and reincarnation have in common?" Lamia asked.

"No," Elias replied, standing up. "I'm not a Buddhist."

"They are all death. Some people think that the final death comes with enlightenment, because people no longer need to be reborn—but enlightenment doesn't lead to death, even if it appears to."

Elias nodded. "Good to know. Thanks for loaning me your knife."

"What I'm saying is, don't be afraid of death. Even if you fail, even if the boy dies and you lose everything, don't get angry and discouraged. Grieve, but don't fall back into darkness because something bad happened. That's attachment, and attachments keep you from enlightenment. Just do your best."

"I'm not trying to become enlightened," Elias said.

Lamia smiled. "You are. Everyone is. They just don't realize it yet."

11

Elias passed the rest of the night quietly in his office, listening for sounds of movement within the building. Nothing out of the ordinary happened that night; Dayna was away, and when Luka woke, Leitha took him into her office and spent much of the night entertaining him. Elias spent some time on his work, but returned several times to where Luka and Leitha sat playing games. Most of the time he paused before reaching the door, listening to Leitha's voice and the occasional sounds of delight from the boy. Curiosity got the better of him, though, and he finally knocked and went in.

"Look who it is!" Leitha said excitedly, pointing to Elias. "What's his name, darling? It's Elias." She glanced up, adding: "He can do it, but I don't know if he knows it's your name." She prodded the child, repeating: "Elias! Elias!"

Luka smiled shyly. He looked from Elias to Leitha and covered his mouth.

"What are you doing, silly?" Leitha asked.

Luka lowered his hands. "Eliot," he said quietly.

Leitha clapped her hands. "Oh, good job, darling, I knew you could do it! You're learning so many things lately."

As Elias watched them, he felt an initial sensation of warmth that quickly turned into dread. Every night, the realization emerged a little more clearly: Luka must have family out there somewhere. He certainly did not belong with Bruno.

He could die here. He could actually die, right here, tonight.

Elias withdrew into the hallway and stood with his back against the wall. Somewhere in the fuzzy realm of his memory was his complaint to Aarya: *People knew something was wrong, but no one did anything.*

He could hear Bruno's off-key singing in the TV room. Bruno had spent little time on his work as of late; his main activities consisted of making noise and eating in front of the TV. Tonight he was his usual loud and obnoxious self, but a bit more forceful and annoying. The moon was on the cusp of fullness, and at such times the werewolf became restless; he shouted rather than spoke, ran rather than walked, and utterly refused to bathe, filling the complex with odor and noise.

Morning arrived without further trouble, and Elias slept. He didn't see Aarya in the evening; she had another obligation at the monastery, which she had invited Elias to attend—a teaching on something called "Tara." It seemed like a tempting alternative to dealing with Bruno on the night of the full moon, but even with his lofty goal of becoming a decent human, Elias didn't feel that he fit in.

He also found lectures on moral and spiritual matters to be tiresome. Nevertheless, he drove to the abbey toward the end of the session and sat in his car, looking at the lit-up windows of the cabins and debating whether to go in.

Instead, he turned the car around and went to the fancy grocer, where he picked out some fruit and a muffin. At the little park where he and Aarya had locked their intentions in place, Elias set up his breakfast up on the flat rock, sticking Aarya's earphones into his ears and humming along with her "Relax" playlist as he ate.

Afterwards he lay on his back, looking up at the cloudless sky, at the stars whose brilliance was dampened by the glowing moon. Elias checked his phone; the park was closing (or so Aarya would say, even though there was no one around to close it). He picked up his litter and made ready to leave. The music had taken a brooding turn anyway: A woman's voice urged love in the face of fear, since death was coming anyway.

"Not sure that qualifies as 'relaxing,'" Elias muttered. He switched off the player and headed for home.

A feeling of dread filled him as he pulled into the parking lot of the business center. Several cars were parked there. Elias recognized none of them, and it was far too late for anyone to have gone to the wrong business office by mistake.

He went through the doors and was blasted by the sour, sweaty smell of cooked ham. Music blasted throughout the complex, and the noise was peppered by sounds of raucous laughter and loud chatter. Elias went to the kitchen, and there was Bruno at the oven, checking on a large smoked ham. Behind him, Luka sat at the dining table. He was flanked by a young woman in a long blue dress and an old man with a sagging, rumpled face. Two women sat across from them. One was small and gray-haired, with long, skinny arms, a deeply wrinkled face, and ice-blue eyes. The other was short and heavy, her brown face marred by old scars; she sat with a smile plastered on her face, chuckling at nothing in particular.

A half-eaten pancake was on the table in front of Luka. The boy ripped off a small piece and shoved it in his mouth, and cast an uneasy look at the woman in the blue dress. She had an arm around his shoulders and was playfully pulling at a lock of his hair.

"Almost done," Bruno said, and spotted Elias in the doorway. "Oh, look who's here." He gestured to Elias and announced: "This is our soon-to-be ex-roommate. He can show you around his digs."

"What the hell are you doing?" Elias seethed.

"Having a little housewarming. Come in and meet your potential replacements. That's Chester and Baubas over there by the kid. And that's Fiura and Baba . . . what's your name again?"

The skinny-armed woman looked at Elias with a sweet smile. "Babaroga," she replied.

"Babaroga." Bruno raised his eyebrows at Elias. "Cute, isn't she? Quit your glaring. There's going to be some new rules around here. Two people on each wing instead of one, for starters. I'm tired of wasting money on rooms I never use."

"Bruno," Elias started.

"There's a nice smoked ham in the oven if you're hungry—oh, but you don't like pork, do you?" Bruno grinned at the guests. "He says it smells like an armpit."

The old man and the large woman chortled.

"Well, there's plenty of armpit to go around," Bruno said. "Be grateful that I'm trying to fill everyone's bellies. It's our wild night. If our guests decide to take a bite out of anyone, it's gonna be you, my wimpling vampire friend."

A sound of breaking glass caught Elias' attention. He withdrew into the hall, looking toward the source. The door to the health lab was open. Light spilled into the hallway, interrupted by the shadows of people moving within.

Elias had made it halfway to the lab when a voice stopped him.

"Elias," it hissed.

He turned around. Dayna was there, coming toward him, watching him with her frigid eyes. Elias heard her draw in a breath, and then her voice came low and coarse: "What is it?"

"I'm a little busy right now, Dayna. I'll have to get

140

back to you." Elias strode away.

Bruno had connected the Bluetooth speakers in the laboratory, so that the sound of Isreal Kamakawiwi`ole singing "Hi`ilawe" blasted through the room, providing a mellow contrast to the chaotic scene inside. A vampire and two other monsters were rifling through cabinets and drawers. The door to the refrigeration unit stood open, and a glass specimen tube lay broken on the floor. It still contained a trace of Elias' latest blood sample, which one of the monsters had presumably consumed.

He stood there for a moment, listening to the other sounds in the building, trying to count monsters and keep track of their whereabouts. Elias walked past his rooms, still listening intently. It wasn't until he reached Leitha's bedroom that he sensed another stranger within. She was inside, and not alone.

Elias turned the knob and found it locked, so he took a step back and kicked the door. It burst open on the first blow. Leitha was on the bed, still dressed in her usual tank top and short shorts, and beside her was a balding, middle-aged man in silk boxers and an unbuttoned shirt. His corpse-like pallor suggested an inhuman, supernatural existence, but one with little energy, certainly not worth Leitha's efforts to use up and drain—but she was likely after his money. The man's pants and shoes had been discarded on the floor beside the bed, and Elias could see the bulge of a wallet in his pants pocket.

Leitha yelped when Elias burst inside, while the man scrambled to sit upright.

"Excuse me, sir," Elias said. "You need to leave now."

"Elias," Leitha protested.

The man gave him a challenging look. "Says who?" the man asked. "I'm not done yet."

"She's my little sister," Elias replied.

The man gaped at him. He looked from Leitha's black

skin to Elias' ghastly white flesh, and he laughed. "Sure she is. You're about as related as a whale and a giraffe."

"Leitha is seventeen," Elias said, his voice descending into a low snarl.

"Bollocks. I've seen her around half the bars and clubs in the city."

"You have," Elias said, "because she has a fake ID. But now you know she's a minor. And I have a special hatred for people who prey on children."

"Do you?" The man began to stand up from the bed. "And what are you—"

Elias lunged and sneered at him with a wide-open mouth, exposing his sharp canines; he grabbed the edge of his open coat and spread it around him like a cape in the wind—a strategy that he used to make himself look larger, to give the effect that darkness had exploded around the specter of his ghastly white face with its raging eyes and deadly fangs.

The man made a strange sound in his throat, a half-cry, half-choking sound. He grabbed his clothes from the floor and ran.

Leitha was still on the bed, her hands splayed behind her. "What the hell did you do that for?" she shouted. "He had money, Elias."

"Stay here," Elias replied, "and lock the door. Don't open it for anyone but me." He started away, but had a sudden thought. "Or Luka," he said. "Don't open it for anyone but me or Luka."

He slammed the door and went back down the hall, hoping that Leitha would heed his advice, though it wasn't really for her safety that Elias wanted her shut away. He simply didn't want her to see what he was doing.

The astra was sheathed in his pocket. Elias kept his hand on it as he checked the rest of the building. The guests had kept to the lab and the kitchen—seven in all, as far as he could tell.

Back at the lab, Elias stood in the doorway and tried not to look frightened. The other monsters were taller than him (though not necessarily more muscular), and their eyes glowed with a wildness that Elias had never seen in his own eyes, even on his worst nights.

Bruno's Hawaiian music was still playing over the speakers. Elias shouted over it: "Excuse me."

The vampire, a tall, dark man in a long coat, turned and sneered at him. "You're excused."

"Party's over," Elias said. "Get out of my house. Now. And don't come back."

Elias stepped back, giving them space to comply. The other two men—zombies, by the degraded look of their bodies—didn't move, but the vampire smiled and moved toward Elias. "Your house, is it?" he asked. He looked Elias slowly up and down; his gaze landed on Elias' bandaged arm, and he inhaled sharply. "You must be the vampire who's on your way out. The *so-called* vampire. That was your blood in the vial, wasn't it?"

Elias' hand shifted in his pocket, sliding the astra from its sheath.

"The werewolf says you're losing your edge . . . but maybe all you need is someone to sharpen it for you." The vampire's grin widened, exposing the points of his teeth.

"It would be better for everyone," Elias said, "if you left now."

The vampire didn't agree. He sneered and came at Elias, pausing only when Elias withdrew the astra. The small silver blade glowed in the overhead light, catching the vampire's attention—but the creature looked at it and laughed. "What is that?" He laughed again. "Is that a cosplay knife? Were you going to stab me with that?"

Elias didn't reply. He simply waited.

The vampire came at him again. With a quick movement, Elias slashed at the creature's hand. He watched as the vampire's mouth opened wide, seemingly in a laugh—but the gleeful look vanished from the creature's eyes, replaced by one of shock. The pale flesh took on a grayish hue, and the veins stood out on the face. The creature slumped stiffly to the floor, eyes and mouth still gaping.

The other two monsters came forward to examine the collapsed figure. Bruno's playlist was between songs, and for a moment, all was quiet. Then the intro to "Hawaiian Wedding Song" started up, seeming to startle the creatures out of their stupor. Their faces contorted with rage—or so it seemed. One's lips had rotted away, so that he was already baring his teeth; the other only had one remaining eye, but it seemed to burn with a newly kindled rage. In a moment that struck Elias as frighteningly surreal, Andy Williams began to sweetly croon about romance and marriage as the zombies lunged with outstretched, rotting hands.

Elias had been wrong about the number of guests. Even before the zombies came into the hall, he could see other figures emerging from the bathrooms. The small crowd watched as the two monsters reared back at the touch of the astra, shrieking and falling to the floor with matching thumps. They froze, looking on with seeming shock; then, with rage in their eyes, they came sprinting down the hall toward Elias.

He walked to meet them, trying to keep his hand from trembling. *Nothing hard about this,* he thought. *Just go for the skin, and you'll be fine.*

Although he had a couple of near misses, the other monsters fell in the same way, with wide-open eyes and agonized snarls and howls.

The crowd in the kitchen was oblivious to the goings-on in the hall. Bruno had heightened the noise with an electric kitchen knife, with which he was lopsidedly slicing the ham, and his own bellowing voice as he screamed the lyrics to "Tiny Bubbles."

Another monster had joined them. He sat at the far end of the table: a large, hairy figure, his face mostly covered by a thick mustache and beard, exposing only his small eyes and yellow teeth. Elias' gaze fixed on Baubas, the young-looking woman who still sat with a finger twined in Luka's hair. She grabbed a lock of it and gave a sharp tug, causing Luka to cry out in protest.

Elias walked around to where the two of them sat. "Let him go," he said to the woman. "I'm taking him with me."

Bruno looked over his shoulder. He stopped the electric knife and set it on the counter. "What'd you say?"

"I said," Elias replied patiently, "that I'm taking Luka." His gaze stayed fixed on Baubas, who looked back at him defiantly. "And if you don't get your scrawny fingers out of his hair right now, I'm going to cut them off."

Baubas exposed her teeth, letting out a quiet hiss.

"I'll be damned if you're taking him anywhere, you little punk." Bruno went to his laptop at the end of the counter and switched the music off. "He's mine. What gives you the right to take him?"

Elias ignored him. "I said *now*," he told Baubas.

Baubas looked up at him with a self-satisfied smile. She gave Luka's hair another tug.

A moment later, the astra slashed against her fingers. Baubas yanked her hand back and stared at it.

The crowd around the table stared, too; then they began to laugh, belching murmurs of mocking laughter.

A look of glee came into Baubas' eyes, and her mouth opened wide, as if she was also about to break into laughter—but the look quickly turned to terror, and she made a sudden, strangled gasp, as though her throat had constricted and cut off her air supply. Her arms went stiff, and she fell sideways out of her chair, landing on the floor with a loud thud.

Bruno gaped. He crouched, looking under the table at the fallen figure.

"Get out," Elias said to the others.

Chester and Babaroga jumped up from their seats and scuttled through the entryway. The hairy man looked indecisively from Elias to Bruno.

"Now," Elias insisted, and the creature slowly left the room.

Bruno stood up. "What the hell did you do to her?"

"She's in shock." Elias crouched down and felt the woman's pulse. It still beat, though it had gone faint, and her breath wheezed in and out of her open mouth.

Luka watched him silently, his eyebrows drawn in a vague expression of worry. Elias stood and picked the child up. "Don't worry, she's just asleep," he said. "Bruno will find a more comfortable place for her to lie down. Won't you, Bruno?"

Luka peered over his arm, trying to get a look at Baubas.

Bruno followed the others into the hall, and found the lobby empty. "You dimwit. Thanks a lot. Now . . . ." He turned around and stopped, seeing the other figures strewn on the floor near the lab. "What the hell, Elias!"

"You can check to see if they're still alive," Elias said. "Be careful, though. They might be a little cranky when they wake up."

The werewolf bellowed: "*I* can check?"

Elias stepped out into the hall. "Yes, Bruno, you can check. You made this mess. Clean up after yourself for once."

Bruno's face filled with rage. Spittle flew from his mouth as he shouted: "You arrogant little brat! I've had it with you!"

"Don't," Elias warned, but the werewolf raised one meaty hand to strike Elias' head; the blow missed its target as Elias stepped back. With his free hand, Elias drove the astra blade into Bruno's forearm.

The werewolf went perfectly still. He, too, seemed to smile gleefully for a moment. Then he fell, and the hall shook with the impact.

Luka had been facing away, looking over Elias' shoulder, but now he turned and scanned the hallway for Bruno. He saw the werewolf lying stiffly on the floor, and he looked at Elias with confusion in his eyes.

"Yeah . . . your dad's sleeping, too," Elias said. "He's fine. Let's go find Leitha, okay?"

He had just begun walking when a sound stopped him: a scuttling in the walls, fast and heavy, like a giant rodent. Elias tried to follow the movements with his eyes; they shifted from the right-hand wall to the ceiling, and then ceased.

Elias moved quietly, keeping his eyes on the spot where the noises had stopped. After a few steps he quickened his pace.

A fragment of ceiling exploded above him.

Elias stumbled back against the wall, watching as bits of plaster fell to the floor. A six-inch hole had been punched in the ceiling. Elias looked for movement within it, but saw only darkness. Slowly, he began to move again.

A scraping sounded in the wall behind him. As Elias glanced toward it, a fist punched through the plaster—a small, bony, wrinkled fist. I appeared only for a moment, and then withdrew.

Luka saw it, too, and made a perturbed sound. "We're

okay," Elias said, still watching the hole.

He shifted Luka in his arms and pulled the astra from his pocket, holding it in front of him.

The building was silent. Elias turned around, checking up and down the hall—and then Luka cried out, and Elias felt the boy yanked upwards.

A long, skinny arm had reached through the hole in the ceiling, stretching down to the child in an impossibly long reach, as though it was made of rubber. The bony fingers clutched the back of the boy's shirt, and the rubbery arm jerked as the creature tried to pull him from Elias' arms.

In a panicked move, Elias grabbed onto the boy with both hands, and in doing so dropped the astra.

Elias glanced at the floor. He couldn't reach the knife without releasing Luka. He yanked on the arm with his free hand, to no effect—so he sank his teeth into the rubbery flesh, biting hard, tearing with his teeth. A shriek sounded from above; the arm thrashed in Elias' mouth. He released it, and it was drawn back up into the ceiling.

Elias spit onto the floor. He bent to pick up the knife, but was stopped by the lightning-quick movement of the other arm; it shot through the hole in the ceiling and embedded its fingers in Luka's shirt.

In a swift movement, Elias pulled the shirt over the boy's head. He grabbed the creature's wrist before Luka could get completely free, keeping a firm hold as he set the boy on the floor.

For a few seconds he engaged in a tug-of-war with the monstrous arm. Elias tried to reach for the astra, but every time he took his hand from the rubbery arm, it yanked so fiercely that he nearly lost his grip. Above him, the creature shrieked in frustration. Its face became visible as it sneered at him through the jagged opening, and Elias recognized the ice-blue eyes and haggard face of

Babaroga.

Luka stood by the wall, watching with wide eyes. "Luka," Elias said. "Hand me that knife, will you?" He grunted as Babaroga gave another fierce pull. "Right there. Pick it up and give it to me."

The boy looked at the astra. He picked it up, not by the handle, but by the blade, and stood looking at it.

"Give it here, Luka," Elias said.

Babaroga's other arm shot through the opening. She grasped Elias by the hair, pulling and tearing, and then gave him a couple of hard slaps on the head, shrieking along with her movements.

Elias tried to grab at her other hand, but it eluded him. "Luka," he said.

The boy lifted the astra in his hands, and Elias made a quick grab at the handle. A moment later, the blade made contact with Babaroga's flesh. The sounds of shrieking came to a sudden halt; the arms, too, went still. Elias heard a hoarse, wheezing breath from above, and then all was silent.

Elias stepped back, panting. The arms that dangled before him turned a sickly shade of gray. Slowly, they began to shrink toward the ceiling, only stopping when they had returned to their former length. Elias glanced up at Babaroga's lifeless blue eyes, and then looked down at Luka. "Good job."

He was about to take the boy's hand when he noticed yet another figure in the hall. Dayna stood beside Bruno's motionless body. Her head was tipped slightly forward so that her hair fell close around her face, disguising the wideness of her mouth and the bleakness of her eyes.

"Dayna," Elias said, still somewhat breathlessly. "We've had . . . a bit of an incident with Bruno's guests."

Dayna lifted her head. Her gaze flicked to Luka. She began to move closer, slowly and without making a sound, staring at the boy with quiet intensity.

Elias stepped in front of Luka and held the astra aloft. "Dayna, please stop right there," he said. "I'm a little freaked out right now, and I don't want anyone coming close to me."

In a low voice, Dayna said: "I'll take him off your hands."

Elias shook his head. "No, you won't."

The wendigo stepped closer. Her chin lifted a little, and she drew in a long, rasping breath. "What is it?" she asked.

"I don't know what that means, Dayna."

She moved another step, leaving little more than a yard between herself and Elias. "What you have . . . I want all of it."

"What do I have that you don't?"

As soon as Elias asked the question, he knew. *A wendigo perceives things like love, happiness, and hope as the richest foods. They crave those things with obsessive desperation, and when they find them, they devour them—but they don't know how to create those feelings themselves, and so they are never sated.*

"Luka," Elias said, "Go and get Leitha." He stepped back, waving the boy away. "Go on. It's hide-and-seek. Leitha is hiding in her room. Go find her, quick."

The boy started down the hall.

The wendigo watched him go. Her gaze flicked back to Elias, and she took another step forward.

"Don't, Dayna," Elias said. "You can't have him. No one is going to hurt that boy."

"I want it," she replied huskily. "Where is it?"

"Where's what?"

She came closer, moving around to Elias' side. "Stop," he said, but Dayna didn't stop, and so he made a quick gesture with the astra—but the wendigo knocked it out of his hand. The knife went flying down the hall, back toward the lobby doors.

Elias grasped his wrist where Dayna had struck him, gasping in pain.

"Where is it?" Dayna rasped.

He took a step back.

"It's not at the abbey," she said.

Elias froze. "What?" he asked, even as the meaning of those words began to sink in.

"It's not at the abbey," Dayna repeated. "Where is it? I want it."

Elias paused. "What do you want?"

As he backed away toward the lobby, Dayna began to open her ghastly mouth. It was a slow process, each moment more horrifying than the next, as the thin lips parted to reveal a long row of large razor-sharp teeth—and behind that, yet another row. Dayna's head seemed to expand in size, the eyes and nose shrinking away behind the massive jaw.

Elias ran.

He made it as far as the astra, even picked it up in his aching hand, but the wendigo simply knocked it away again. It clattered against the wall and fell to the ground, and Dayna stepped between Elias and the knife, cutting off his route.

"Give it to me," she said in a whispery voice, "or I will eat it off of you."

Elias' mind raced for a strategy. "Can't we talk this out?" he asked. "We had kind of a nice setup here. We should try to save what's left of it."

She came toward him, and he backed into the kitchen, looking around for something else to use as a weapon. The colossal mouth was opening again, exposing a multitude of deadly teeth.

Elias grabbed a pan from the stove, but Dayna didn't

stop—and when he tried to strike her with it, she simply grabbed it from him and threw it to the floor.

A coffee mug sat on the counter; Elias threw that, too, followed by a couple of empty beer bottles, but Dayna easily ducked out of their paths, and they shattered behind her.

Elias reached for something else. The smoked ham still sat there, and he picked it up in desperation as Dayna's fingers clasped around his throat.

"Where is it?" she asked. "I . . . WANT . . . IT!"

He struck her with the ham, holding it fast in both hands. Dayna grunted as the slab of meat made contact with her jaw. Elias hit her again. She grabbed the ham and yanked it from his grasp—and then the mouth was opening wide again, and Elias was hit with the foul blast of the wendigo's breath. The smell of decay, that he had so often tried to chase from the air around Dayna's rooms, struck Elias full on as the wendigo exhaled into his face— and then she drew in a loud, rasping breath, and Elias felt something being sucked from him, as through the wendigo's breath had permeated his soul and was now being drawn back into her lungs, dragging his spirit and his livelihood with it.

"It's not at the abbey," she said again. "It's at a house. Where is it?"

Elias' right hand reached for the counter, desperately searching. His fingers closed around the handle of the electric knife.

The buzz of the knife must have startled the wendigo; she relaxed her grip, and Elias lifted the knife and slashed at her face, making a large gash along the side of her mouth. She snarled at him and grabbed his throat again. Elias grabbed her wrist with his free hand, trying to pull it loose as he drove the knife into Dayna's arm.

She screamed and tried to claw at his eyes. Elias

152

moved his head back and forth, trying to avoid her fingernails. He didn't let go of her arm until the knife had cut it completely off.

Dayna let out a blood-curdling shriek and fled from the room. Elias stood there, watching, and finally turned off the knife. He set it quietly on the counter. His arms, his clothes, were soaked with Dayna's blood. The lifeless arm lay on the floor at his feet.

Elias realized that he was shaking. He moved slowly, making his way out of the kitchen, through shards of glass and jagged chunks of ceramic.

Footsteps sounded in the hallway. Elias picked up one of the ceramic pieces, ready to use it as a weapon, but was relieved to see Leitha in the entryway.

She gaped at the mess in the kitchen and Elias' bloody figure. "Christ, Elias! What the hell is going on?"

"Where's Luka?" Elias asked. Still trembling, he went into the hall. The astra still lay where it had fallen.

"I don't know. Whose arm is that?"

"It's Dayna's." Elias stooped to pick up the knife. "She was going to hurt Luka."

"What?"

"Help me find him, Leitha, or he's going to die." Elias hurried past her, checking both halls and finding them empty except for the motionless bodies still strewn around the floor. A trail of blood spatters led down the hall toward Dayna's corner of the building. Elias turned to Leitha, debating whether to send her to look for Luka on her own.

"Stay close to me," he said instead. "She's in a rage. I'm afraid she'll hurt you."

"Elias, what the hell happened?" She pointed to Bruno. "What's wrong with everyone?"

"Let's find Luka," he replied, "and then I'll explain everything."

They followed the trail to Dayna's rooms. It disappeared into an unused room just around the corner, and Elias knew even before reaching it that a window had been opened; the chill of the night air had begun to permeate the hall, and he could hear a light breeze rustling the dry autumn leaves of the oak tree outside.

A check of the room revealed Dayna's blood smeared along the sill and the wall below. Elias detected traces of her foul smell along with the coppery scent of blood.

"I don't think she has Luka," Elias said. "Let's split up and look for him. I'll look in Bruno's rooms. You check our side of the building."

Leitha went around the back. Elias followed as far as Bruno's corner and checked the rooms one by one, making his way toward the front. He was in a corner room of the business complex when he heard a light banging sound in the lobby area—the sound of a door closing.

Elias went to the lobby and looked through the glass doors. A tall streetlamp illuminated the parking lot in front of the building. It was empty, but Elias caught sight of a blood smear on the door handle, and of droplets along the carpet that led outside.

"Shit," he said.

He moved quietly, first peeking into the kitchen. It was empty except for the still-unconscious Baubus—but Elias looked again and noticed something missing. Dayna's arm was no longer on the kitchen floor.

He could hear Leitha's voice; she was talking in that sweet, enthusiastic tone she only used with Luka. Elias stepped back into the hall and let out a relieved sigh as he saw her coming down the hall with the boy in her arms.

"Found him in my bedroom," she said.

"Okay. Good."

Luka stared at Elias, at his blood-soaked clothes and spattered face.

"Maybe I'll just take him back to my room," Leitha said.

"Do that. I'll go with you."

He hurried them toward Leitha's bedroom, where they made a quick check of the closet and other spaces, and found them empty. "Stay here," Elias advised her, "and lock the door. Don't open it to anyone but me."

"Fine, Elias, but what are you going to do?"

"I'm going to find Dayna. If she's not after Luka, I'm afraid . . . ." He paused. "She has another person she's targeting."

"Who?" Leitha asked.

"My nun friend."

"Why would Dayna target her?"

Elias stepped into the hall. "I'll explain all of this later. Just stay safe, and keep Luka safe. Lock this as soon as I close it. And find something you can use as a weapon."

Elias shut the door and headed for the parking lot, the astra gripped firmly in his hand.

12

Elias found the parking lot still empty and quiet. The trail of blood droplets led to the back of the lot, toward a row of red pines. Elias heard a sound coming from somewhere beyond them—a wet, sloppy sound, one he couldn't identify at first, but as he moved closer it brought to mind an image of Bruno eating a barbecued chicken wing, smacking his lips and licking the sauce from his fingers. Elias moved past the trees and caught sight of a figure crouching on the other side. Dayna sat there, facing him. Her clothes were soaked with blood, and even with her head lowered, Elias could see her teeth gleaming in the full moonlight. She raised something to her gaping mouth, tearing off a section and chewing.

Elias could see fingers protruding from the hunk of meat in Dayna's hands. He realized that she was eating her own arm.

He stumbled backwards, covering his mouth and making a small sound of horror.

The wendigo looked up. She lowered the piece of flesh in her hands, giving Elias a full view of her gaping, bloody mouth. Dayna hissed at him, a loud, outraged sound—and then she ran, fleeing toward the road.

Elias heard the slapping of her bare feet against the pavement. He watched, stunned, as the wendigo disappeared in the direction of town.

He hurried to his car. His jacket was still on, with the keys in his pocket; he fumbled for them, dropped them, and tried again.

A minute later he was driving down the road with his brights on, scanning his surroundings for any sign of the wendigo. At the first stop sign he thought he caught sight of a movement in the rearview mirror—but he looked again, twisted around in his seat, and saw nothing.

He drove on, haunted by the wendigo's words: *It's at a house. Where is it?*

It was possible, he thought, that she might know about the house where Aarya lived. Dayna might have sucked the knowledge of it from his mind, the same way she had seemingly tried to suck out his soul.

The house was a twelve-minute drive from the business center. Elias looked at the digital clock again and again, assuring himself that even if Dayna knew where the house was, she wouldn't be able to beat him there. When he pulled up in the driveway, he found the quaint two-story house looking the same as he had left it, with its clean-swept porch and messages of welcome. The windows were shaded, but Elias could see that the light was on in Aarya's bedroom and in the living room. He hurried to the front door and knocked, still gripping the astra in his hand.

Seconds passed. Elias knocked again, impatiently, calling out: "Aarya!"

He glanced over his shoulder, looking at the street, and saw it empty. As he turned toward the door, though, a sudden dread filled his being. He had seen something—not in the street, but a peculiar shape on the roof of his car.

Elias looked over his shoulder again.

The porch light flicked on, illuminating the driveway, where Dayna lay spread-eagled on top of Elias' car. Her one remaining hand still clutched at the passenger-side roof. She stared at Elias and didn't move.

The front door opened. Aarya stood there in pajama

pants and a T-shirt, her eyes full of alarm as she looked at Elias' bloody, disheveled appearance. "Elias! What—"

"Get inside," Elias snapped. He shoved past her, slamming the door shut as the wendigo leapt onto the porch.

The force of Dayna's body rattled the door. Elias hurried to lock it, first the knob, and then the thin, useless-looking chain, before turning to Aarya. He looked her over and let out a relieved breath.

"You're safe," he said, and hugged her.

She didn't hug him back. "Elias. Elias, you're covered in blood." Aarya pulled back. "What happened? Are you okay?"

"Yeah. It's Dayna's blood. Mostly."

Dayna's body thumped against the door again, followed by the sound of a snarl.

"Dayna, your roommate?" Aarya asked. "Is that her?"

"Yes, that's her." He looked around the room, and called out: "Beth!"

"She's not here," Aarya said.

Elias placed a hand against the door. "What kind of wood is this?"

"I don't know. Why is your roommate here, and why is she trying to break down the door?"

"I think she wants to eat you." Elias pulled on Arya's arm, guiding her toward the stairs. "I'm sorry, but I accidentally brought her here. I was trying to protect you."

"Where are we going?"

"Upstairs. Where's your cell phone?"

"In my room."

"Get it," Elias commanded her, "and then lock yourself in the bathroom."

Aarya stopped him. "What, by myself? What are you going to do?"

"I'll handle her."

Danya body-slammed the door again, and Aarya shook her head. "No, let me help," she said.

"You can't. I have to use this on her." Elias held up the astra.

"Why, what is that?"

"I'll explain later. Just get your phone and do what I say, please. Trust me on this one."

The bedroom lamp was on. Aarya had left a book open on the bedspread, with her phone beside it. She picked up the phone and hesitated. "Maybe I should call the police," she said uncertainly, looking again at Elias' blood-stained clothes.

"Not yet. Only do that as a last resort, if she gets into the house. Okay? A cop won't be able to stop her."

Elias' own words made him doubt. If something happened to him, and if Dayna got into the house, a cheap bathroom door wouldn't hold her off. By the time anyone responded to Aarya's call, it would be too late.

As he stood there debating, he heard the living room window exploding in a shower of glass. The shards tinkled across the laminate floor, and mixed in with that sound was the padding of Dayna's feet and a few grunts and snarls of pain.

Elias couldn't conceal the fear in his eyes. "Stay behind me," he said, and went to the doorway.

The wendigo was nearly at the top of the stairs. Dayna saw Elias and froze. Her cold, snake-like eyes flicked to the bedroom doorway, and she moved up another couple of steps, leaving a pair of bloody footprints behind her.

Elias didn't bother talking. He held the astra and waited.

"It's there," Dayna whispered, and placed her foot on the last step. Her eyes fixed momentarily on Elias, and for the first time he thought he saw a flicker of emotion there—something like wonder. "What is it?" she asked.

Slowly, she ascended into the hall, moving toward Elias with smooth, bloody steps. Her left forearm, Elias realized, was longer than when he had last seen it; a thin protuberance, fleshy and wet, had grown out of the wound, and the skin itself had healed over the bone. Elias' gaze drifted down to the end of the nub, and there he could see a set of tiny fingers, rubbery and translucent— and he realized that her arm was growing back.

He lunged, thinking that even if he missed Dayna with the astra, he might at least push her down the stairs.

She grabbed his wrist, avoiding the blade. Elias threw the weight of his body into her; Dayna released him and stumbled backwards, careening past the top of the steps down the hard, wooden steps.

She crouched low and caught the railing with her good hand, stopping her fall.

Elias swore under his breath. "Please, Dayna, just stop."

"I want it," Dayna rasped, straightening up.

She leapt at him, slamming his hand against the wall and jarring the knife from his grip. Dayna kicked at the handle with her bloody foot, sending it clattering down the stairs. With her one arm, she grabbed Elias and threw him in the same direction.

The wendigo, thin and meager as she was, was no weakling. Elias nearly toppled down the stairs, but managed to stop himself, landing face-down at the edge of the staircase with his hands splayed on the steps below.

The wendigo was in the bedroom with Aarya. Elias heard something—Aarya, he presumed—being shoved against a wall, so hard that it must have knocked the crucifix from its place. Elias heard it fall to the floor.

He scrambled to his feet, pausing in fearful indecision: should he go after the astra, or after the monster?

His indecisiveness only lasted a moment. Elias hurried to the bedroom and found Aarya sitting on the floor, her back against the wall and Dayna's fingers around her throat. Aarya had grabbed the crucifix from the floor.

"That," Dayna said in her rasping voice, "won't work on me."

Aarya stabbed the long end of the crucifix into the wendigo's eye.

Dayna shrieked as Aarya stabbed at her again and again—but she didn't release her grip. She tore the crucifix from Aarya's hand just as Elias rammed into her. Dayna sprawled, and quickly struggled to her feet.

Elias rammed her again. He pushed with all his might, trying to slam her so hard that every bone in her body would break, hard enough to punch through the far wall, or to punch right through to another dimension—as far away from Aarya as he could take her.

The two crashed through the bedroom window. Elias realized with a strain of panic that he and Dayna were falling—that they were hurtling toward the ground in a cloud of jagged glass.

He landed on top of the wendigo, his face ramming into her massive jaw. Elias rolled off of her, and for several seconds he found himself unable to draw a breath. He saw sharp bursts of light before his eyes, like tiny fireworks, probably a result of hitting his forehead; they flickered and faded, allowing Elias a view of the night sky.

For a moment, he felt tempted to stay there. Elias struggled to draw in one breath, and then another. The fall had jarred his lower back, and his head seared with pain. Weakly, he reached beside him.

His fingers met slick fragments of glass and tiny shards that cut his flesh, but the wendigo was gone.

With a moan, Elias forced himself to sit up. Dayna

161

was nowhere in sight. Elias stumbled to the living room window, clumsily making his way over the frame and into the house, slicking the frame with his blood. Beth's porch sign lay in the middle of the room among the glass, entreating guests to sit, talk, and laugh; Dayna had used it to break the window.

The wendigo was crouched strangely near the stairs, facing the wall. Elias started toward her, trying to ignore the pain in his body, to force his lungs to keep drawing air in and out. He was in such a sorry state that he had forgotten about the astra. He would have missed it completely, but the knife was lying directly in his path, only a foot or two behind the wendigo.

Elias tried to creep in silence, hoping to take Dayna by surprise—but he gasped as he realized that Dayna was not alone. Aarya sat against the wall, in much the same position as before. The wendigo's head tipped back as the mouth opened; the jaw dropped low, the eyes and nose dipping back at a strange angle to make way for the giant maw. Dayna exhaled onto Aarya, a foul-smelling wind that blanched Aarya's face and made her writhe in disgust.

After a moment, though, Aarya's face relaxed. She lifted her left hand, palm up, above her lap; she lowered her right hand to the ground.

Elias reached for the astra. His hand ached, and the movement was a clumsy one; the knife slid against the floor as he grasped it.

The wendigo's head turned, and Elias found himself momentarily faced with rows of terrifying teeth and a gorged red throat. Dayna's mouth snapped shut, giving him a momentary glimpse of her eyes: one now bloody and ruined, the other glaring at him with defiant rage. Her breath hit Elias in a pungent blast as she hissed: "It's mine!"

With a quick movement, she drove her teeth into

Aarya's torso, and then turned again to strike at Elias.

Her maneuver, this time, was too slow. Before Dayna could turn around, Elias pushed the astra through her long hair, scraping it along the back of her neck.

The wendigo stiffened. Elias felt a change in the air as the foul breath ceased, and with it, he felt a rush of relief. Dayna fell sideways with a thump, and lay silent and unmoving.

"Aarya," Elias said, scrambling around the body to Aarya's side. "Are you all right?"

Aarya's face was ashen. She sat with one palm still turned toward the ceiling. Her eyes opened, focusing briefly on Elias, and then she jerked as blood spurted from her mouth.

Her clothes were wet with blood. Elias looked down at the red tears in her T-shirt, where Dayna's razor teeth had slashed deep into her flesh. As he watched, blood began to stream down in rivulets, pooling on the floor around Aarya's legs.

She coughed again. Elias pulled off his coat, folding it over and pressing it to the massive wound. "Aarya, hang on," he said, fumbling for his phone with his other hand. "I'm going to get help."

He set the phone on the floor and swiped a finger across the screen. Elias hurriedly entered the lock code; a "wrong pin" message flashed. He tried again, and again, more slowly, with the same result.

Elias swore under his breath. Looking up, he caught a partial view of the kitchen and a cordless phone on the wall.

"I have to get a different phone," he said. Aarya's upraised hand fell limply into her lap, and Elias grabbed it, trying to clasp the fingers around his cell phone. "Hold this . . . ."

He trailed off as he looked at her eyes. Aarya's breath

163

had stopped. Her eyes were half open, but Aarya could no longer be seen in them. The sheen of her spirit had vanished, leaving the brown eyes vacant and unrecognizable.

"Aarya," Elias said. "Wake up. You're in shock." He spoke the words even though he knew they weren't true. He stared helplessly, and almost began to admonish her: *Don't you dare die. You can't.* Instead, a small, choked sob sounded in his throat.

Elias' gaze drifted to Dayna. She lay on her side, the unfinished arm sticking out from beneath her. Elias had a sudden impulse to tear the creature's jaw apart, to smash it into innumerable pieces that could never be regrown— but the jaw had retracted, and the mouth narrowed to the shape of a human mouth. Dayna's eyes, too, had changed. The cold, flat look had receded; the impression of a starved soul was gone.

Elias got to his feet and staggered to the kitchen. He punched the numbers on the phone with numb fingers, turning to face the chaotic scene in the living room—a scene that he could not yet begin to explain. When the dispatcher answered, he only said, "I need help. Please send an ambulance. Two of them."

He carried the phone back to where Aarya's body sat against the wall. Elias set the phone on the floor a few feet away, ignoring the voice on the other end. Dispatch would be able to trace the call, and now there was no reason for help to rush in.

"Aarya," Elias said again, and hoped for a miracle. He put an arm around her, carefully drawing her close until her head rested against his face. Elias inhaled the essence of her, the woods-and-incense scent now mixed with the tang of her blood. "Come back to life," he whispered. "If anyone can do it, you can."

Elias heard the dispatcher speaking to him from the

floor, but he didn't move from his spot. When the paramedics arrived, they would take Aarya's body away. He would never be able to hold her again.

13

The incident, from where it began at the business center and ended at Beth's house, became a high-profile case—and the investigation kept turning up more oddities and unexplained findings. The police subjected Leitha and Elias to several rounds of questioning, initially at the station, and the last few at the business center, where the two so-called monsters worked to clean up the messes that had been left behind.

Elias patiently provided explanations: Bruno had brought Luka home one night, claiming custody of him; Elias had used the lab to study genetic mapping, and had even collected samples from Bruno and Luka to see if they were really father and son; he came home one evening and found a lot of strange people in his house, and they simply passed out where they stood, possibly from a drug that had been passed around; Dayna tried to strangle him and gouge his eyes, and he cut her in panicked self-defense. Later, Elias' skin would be found beneath the fingernails on Dayna's right hand, and news articles stated that the partygoers, now mostly comatose or suffering from amnesia, had exceedingly high levels of "stimulants" in their blood. Dayna's underdeveloped arm was attributed to a genetic aberration; the many cuts on her body, and her excessive blood loss, were attributed to the electric knife and broken glass.

Bruno was among the amnesiacs. Dayna and Babaroga were listed as fatalities in the event. Elias experienced a surreal moment when he saw their full names printed in a local newspaper: Dayna Zonta Smith and Kasmira Bryn Babaroga. The sight of those names reminded Elias that the women had once been human; they had been born, they had been given names, and something about their lives had pulled them into darkness.

It was that same darkness that Elias found himself fighting in the days after Aarya's death.

The reunion with her, and the sudden loss of her, brought him to a new and unique realm of despair. It hung heavy over his waking hours, and in sleep it whispered tales of futility: nightmares in which nothing good survived, but was instead hunted and devoured by darkness. In his dreams, too, came shadowy memories of his mother's death. Elias remembered little about her. His memories maintained a vague impression of his mother's short blond hair and blue eyes, but the rest of her face lacked detail; he only knew her face from old photos. He remembered loving her, being happy with her—and then came the strange days at her bedside in the hospital, where people talked to him about heaven and claimed that his mother was moving on to a better world. Elias watched her become shrunken, pale, and bald. It didn't look like she was going to a better place. But even though he didn't understand, he had time to say goodbye.

In contrast, Aarya's death seemed cruelly abrupt. There had been no last words, no final encouragements or promises, no ceremony, no music. Every time Elias woke to another day, he had to re-convince himself that she was gone. Aarya's parents had taken her remains back to Colorado for the funeral, so there was no grave site for him to visit. He attended a memorial service for her at the monastery, where the nuns and volunteers gave speeches and shared anecdotes, but Elias took little comfort; instead, he fixated on Aarya's absence. There were no photographs at the memorial, and even Aarya's ashes had been taken away.

Lamia assured him that Aarya was very much present, in the way she had affected people and the opportunities she had helped build. Elias tried to share her perspective.

At home, he found an unexpected source of comfort in Leitha. She had seen, with some degree of shock, the magnitude of Elias' grief, and even shared in his sense of loss. When the two of them were brought for questioning, Elias didn't just talk to the police detectives; he sobbed, and was sometimes comforted afterward by Leitha's embrace—a genuine, caring, and mutually heartsore embrace, devoid of her usual flirtation and neediness. When Luka was taken away at the station, Leitha tried to reassure the child, forcing a smile and saying: "It's okay, darling. They're going to help you find your mum," and as soon as he was out of sight, she crumpled into herself and wept. Elias tried to spend time with Leitha at home rather than being alone. When left to himself, he descended easily into a toxic mix of grief and anger—at himself, at the world, at the cosmos that arranged the fates of humans, and even at Aarya. Elias sometimes thought, in the fever of his frustration, that Aarya had somehow done this on purpose—that she had known she was going to die, and had never intended to be with him.

Elias dealt with such feelings in his new ways: going for walks with Aarya's music player, going to the monastery to talk with the nuns. At first, out of guilt, he couldn't face Beth. When he finally worked up the nerve to talk to her, he cried so hard that he couldn't speak.

A wall within him had been town down.

Sometimes, too, Elias went to Cinnabar Park. He walked the trails and stopped at the love lock he shared with Aarya, thinking of her promise that they would be together, even if it took more than a lifetime—even if it was as far away as nirvana. He told himself that he needed only reach it to be with her again.

168

In his darker moments, though, this prospect didn't seem like a promise. It seemed rather like a long-drawn-out torment.

Elias had become a day creature thanks to his new routines. He filled his free time with leaving his unsavory life behind; he had found a new home, and kept himself busy with preparations to exit the office complex. Tidying the space, and making it clean for the next occupants, gave him a sense of closure and newness—a blank slate for things to come.

On the day of his lease signing, Elias walked first to the monastery, where he quietly sat in on the morning's chants and prayers, and then back to the business center. From his office, he retrieved the printout bearing the details of his new home. As he stood reading over the paper, his right hand clutched a pair of keys in his pocket—the brass keys to the love lock. Elias always carried the keys with him, and found himself grasping them often.

The hand that clutched the paper was scratched; the stitches across the back of his wrist had not yet been removed. A few weeks ago, his body would have erased those wounds within a day, smoothing them over with whatever supernatural force had accelerated his body's healing powers. Though some of the cuts still hurt, Elias no longer minded looking at them. He was learning to live with being wounded.

Leitha appeared in the doorway. She clung to the door frame and gave Elias a quick once-over. "Did you walk to the monastery again?"

"I did. I don't recommend it. It's freezing out there."

She shook her head, releasing a barely audible sigh. "I can't believe you, of all people, joined a monastery—or even that you walked into one."

"I haven't joined the monastery. I joined . . . a

community." Elias looked down at the paper in his hand, then folded it and slipped it into his pants pocket. "It's been good for me. I'm . . . angry, and I feel very sorry for myself right now."

"Well, no one's gonna hold it against you."

"I'm disgusted at myself. I feel like I got Aarya killed."

"Dayna killed her. You didn't do a thing. Just let yourself miss her, and don't blame yourself."

Elias looked at Leitha's somber but sympathetic expression. She was wise, in a way, he had come to realize; she was good at comforting others. He thought it unfortunate that she rarely applied her wisdom to her own life.

"You really loved her," Leitha said—but she said it with a note of doubt, as though it was a question rather than on observation.

"I did," Elias said. "I always have. Aarya was the only person I ever wanted to be with, and she was good. It helps me to be around people who knew her, and who sound like her." Elias paused. "Well, they sort of sound like her. No one else is quite as reckless, or as unpredictable. Or as fun." He checked his pockets to make sure he had his wallet and phone. "I'm heading out again in a minute. My lease signing is today."

"Which place did you get?"

"The townhouse. It's a two bedroom, so it's more space than I need, but . . . it's the place where I wanted to live with Aarya. I think I'll feel better if I'm living in a home that I wanted to share with her. I don't know . . . maybe I'm in denial. Like, if I get this place, maybe I'll keep expecting her to show up someday."

Leitha's gaze became suddenly distant. "Funny how that works, isn't it? I keep going into Bruno's room and expecting to see Luka."

Of course, it was unlikely that they would ever see Luka again. The police had located his family, and he was living several hours away with an aunt and uncle. Luka's mother, it turned out, was very much alive, but in no position to raise a child. Elias didn't know the details— only that she had handed the boy off to Bruno in the hopes that he would be better taken care of.

Leitha's mood had been depressed since Luka's departure; his absence left a dispirited slouch in her usually vibrant face.

"You're good with kids," Elias said. "You should get out of this kind of life. Someday, you can find someone to have your own children with."

She scoffed. "Not likely."

"Leitha, why don't you move in with me? There's plenty of space. You could come with me, and we could sign the lease together."

"With *you*?" She took a step back. "And get snapped at, and insulted? I kind of loved you, Elias. You hurt me with the things you said."

"And I meant it when I said I loved you like a little sister. It's not an insult. I don't have family, and Bruno and Dayna were way too messed up to have any kind of relationship to me, but you've been like my family." Elias thought back to the night of the full moon, to the sight of Leitha with the emaciated-looking man, to the feelings of anger it had stirred in him. "And I should have done more to protect you. I do love you, Leitha. You can have something better than all this."

"You think I'm too dumb to find my own way," she replied.

"There is no finding your way in places like this," Elias said, making a wide gesture. "I'm done with this world. I suggest you get out of it, too."

"And go back to what? Lifting my head high and

171

looking up, only to get my face stepped on? I've done that." Leitha's voice began to waver. "It hurts, Elias. At least this way, I already know what to expect."

"If that was true," he replied, "then you couldn't have been hurt by me." He waited for the words to sink in, and entreated her again: "Come live with me."

Leitha looked at him, lips trembling, eyes becoming wet with tears.

"There's more out there than just getting stepped on," Elias said. "There are decent people who are at least trying to do good. There's love out there. Actual love."

She smiled bitterly, shaking her head. "There's not," she said. "You'll find out."

"I suppose I will." He grabbed his wallet and started away, calling over his shoulder: "Let me know if you change your mind."

"Those people at the monastery won't accept you like one of their own," Leitha called after him. "Sanctimonious people like that . . . they're only looking for someone to judge, or to make themselves look good. 'Look at how I fixed this poor, pathetic person.' That's all you'll get."

"That's not what other people have gotten," he called back. "I'll take my chances."

Outside, the air was crisp and cold; autumn was giving way to winter, sending down its first snowflakes, tiny and brittle things that coated the ground like white dust. The dusting swirled around Elias' feet as he strode to his car. He slid halfway into the passenger seat, leaning over to start the engine and switch on the heater, and then stood up again to pull the folded paper from his pants pocket. His gaze swept from the photo in the upper corner, an image of a yellow townhouse with a screened porch, to the address at the bottom.

"Elias," a voice called.

He turned to see Leitha hurrying after him, hastily dressed in an open coat and unlaced boots. She was breathless by the time she caught up, and panted as she spoke. "Let me . . . come with. I'll give the place a look."

Elias smiled at her. "I'm glad."

She slid into the passenger seat next to him. Elias started the car, but made no move to leave. He sat staring at Leitha until she said, "What are you looking at? Did I grow another nose?"

"Seat belt," he prodded her.

She rolled her eyes and pulled on the strap.

"Before we sign anything," Elias said, putting the car into gear, "we have to establish some house rules. Number one: Don't flirt with me. Not even as a joke. It drives me up the wall."

"And no calling you Vlad. Got it."

"Number two: No bringing scummy men to our house."

"Why, what are you going to do? Flap your coat and snarl at them with your vampire teeth?"

"My fangs are disappearing. Look." Elias bared his teeth at her, rubbing a fingertip along one of his canines. "They're turning back into ordinary teeth. And I'm still covered with cuts; no more rapid healing for me."

"That's wicked," Leitha said. "In a bad way."

"It's fine. So, do we agree? No scummy men—not just in the house, but no meeting them in general. Actually, let me rephrase that: No men. Period. You're a minor."

"Not for long," Leitha said. "I'll be eighteen next week."

Elias looked at her in subtle surprise. He hadn't ever considered that his roommates had birthdays, but Leitha's revelation put new thoughts into his head—thoughts of gifts, sweets, and cheesy birthday parties. "Fine," he said. "But if you date anyone, he has to be decent. No married men, no scummy perverts, and no jerks. And no more draining people, and using them, and taking their money. If you break either of those rules, the deal's off."

She let out a harsh sigh. "Off to a great start, aren't we? You're asking a lot."

"I'm really not," he said.

"Do I get to make any rules?"

"Go for it." Elias waited, but Leitha didn't offer any suggestions. "Well?"

"I can't think of anything," she said. "You've been a decent roomie. Just . . . no shouting at me, and no grabbing me. If I do something that bothers you, just tell me."

"I will tell you. Will you listen?"

"I will try," she conceded, and flashed him a small, reluctant grin. "Brother." She chuckled. "That sounds really weird. I so haven't thought of you that way."

As Elias came to the first stop sign, he reached down and started Aarya's "Kinda happy" playlist. It seemed a fitting time to listen. Perhaps she had given him these songs with the idea that they would become a self-fulfilling prophecy: survival and hope first, and then a little bit of happiness, and then, perhaps someday, something greater.

The music began in that mellow guitar style that Aarya seemed to like so much, and then it weaved into other, deeper and lighter tones, a tapestry of inspired sound that projected a little bit of hope into Elias' still-broken heart. The vocals began—something about an orphan jumping a train, having nowhere to go and no one to go to, and yet Elias heard that same sound of hope in the idea of what might come next, and of life itself. He glanced at Leitha and sat looking a few moments at her smile. It was beautiful, and for now, it was enough.

www.ingramcontent.com/pod-product-compliance
Lightning Source LLC
Chambersburg PA
CBHW030957210726
48290CB00007B/2346